BACK TO THE DAY LINCOLN WAS SHOT!

DOANE

BACK TO THE DAY LINCOLN WAS SHOT!

Beatrice Gormley

AN
APPLE
PAPERBACK

SCHOLASTIC INC.
New York Toronto London Auckland Sydney

ISBN 0-590-46228-8

12 11 10 9 8 7 6 5 4 3 2 1   6 7 8 9/9 0 1/0

Printed in the U.S.A.   40

First Scholastic printing, January 1996

CONTENTS

1.
We Changed the Past

Jonathan Schultz and his friend Matt Cowen, both twelve, stood in Matt's driveway. "We're in deep marshmallow," said Matt. His head was down, his hands in his shorts pockets. "I wish we didn't have to wait for Emily. I wish we could go over to Grandpa Frank's now and let him yell at us and get it over with."

Jonathan shifted from one long, skinny leg to the other, but that didn't ease the knot in his stomach. He couldn't enjoy the warmth of the spring afternoon, because he didn't want to face Matt's great-grandfather, Mr. Kenny.

Mr. Kenny wasn't any relation to Jonathan, but he was very important to him. After Jonathan's parents were divorced, years ago, he'd started hanging around Mr. Kenny's workshop with Matt. Then the old man had realized Jonathan had a gift for working with machines, and taken him on as a kind of apprentice.

By now, Jonathan felt like an honorary great-grandson. It was Mr. Kenny, not Dad, who had come to the sixth-grade science fair last fall to see Jonathan win first prize. But if he was Mr. Kenny's honorary great-grandson, Jonathan worried, could that honor be taken away?

"I can't believe you left the date, 1775, on the clock," Matt said for the third time. "That was a dead giveaway."

Matt was talking about the destination clock on the TASC, the Time and Space Connector. Mr. Kenny had invented the TASC to visit the sinking of the *Titanic* in 1912. If Jonathan had returned the setting of the destination clock to 1912, Mr. Kenny would never have suspected their visit to the American Revolution.

Matt's blue-gray eyes met Jonathan's, and he went on hastily, "Okay, okay. So I could have thought of the clock myself, before we returned the TASC to Grandpa Frank."

"Yeah, you could have," said Jonathan. But actually he blamed himself. He was the only one of the three kids who really understood how the TASC worked, and he was always the one who handled the equipment.

A car pulled into the driveway, and Jonathan and Matt backed out of the way, onto the lawn. "At last," said Matt. "Someone's mom, dropping Emily off."

A back door of the car opened, and a girl with curly red hair wiggled out. She waved thanks

2

to the woman driving the car, pulled down the bottom of her Mets T-shirt, and bounced up to the boys. "You guys! Wait till you hear this."

"Never mind," said Matt to his younger sister. "We have to — "

"This painting!" Emily rushed on. "In the museum. See, I was on a field trip. Anyway, we were supposed to be looking at the modern art, but I just *happened* to see this painting in another room!" She paused, her light blue-green eyes glinting. "A painting from the Revolutionary War. Of the Battle of Lexington!"

"So what?" asked Jonathan.

A laugh bubbled up with Emily's answer. "*So,* one of the Americans is lying in the front part of the picture with a *handkerchief* bandage on his leg. And guess what the initials on the handkerchief are?"

Matt had been sighing impatiently. Now he said, "Who cares? Look, Emily, Grandpa Frank called, and — "

"Matt, listen." Emily pushed her face closer to her brother's. "They were *your* initials; M.A.C. It was your handkerchief, the one you left in 1775!"

That was such a ridiculous conclusion that Jonathan laughed out loud. "Oh, right, as if that's some kind of proof. Anybody could have the same initials as Matt."

"Yeah," said Matt. "In fact, they must have

been the initials of the guy who painted the picture."

"They were not," said Emily. "I checked that. What's the matter with you two? Don't you think it's cool that we changed the past, just a little tiny bit?"

"Don't you think you could *listen* to me?" Matt said severely. "Grandpa Frank found out about our trip to the Revolution. He's really mad. We have to go over there, right now, and let him yell at us." He started down the driveway. "So let's get going."

That didn't shut Emily up right away. As they started off toward Mr. Kenny's neighborhood, she wanted to know how the old man had found out that they'd used his time-travel device, and exactly how mad he was, and whether there was any chance they could ever use the TASC again. But then Emily fell back a few paces, looking unusually serious, and let the boys walk by themselves.

Matt rolled his eyes at Jonathan. "Ever since Emily was in that *Tom Sawyer* play, she's tried to make things more exciting than they really are. Like, that really could have been my handkerchief in that painting."

"Yeah," said Jonathan, relieved to think about something besides how angry Mr. Kenny must be. "She doesn't have a clue about what makes real proof. For the handkerchief to really be scientific proof, we would've had to have seen the painting *without* the handkerchief *before* we traveled to the Revolution. Anyway, we already know that you can't change the past."

As the three kids reached the neighborhood where Mr. Kenny lived, they walked more slowly. In front of his driveway, they paused. To Jonathan, the garage looked like a lion's den. The door of the old man's garage workshop was up, and there he was at his workbench, in well-worn khaki pants and a long-sleeved work shirt.

Squaring her shoulders, Emily marched up the driveway and into the workshop. Jonathan and Matt trailed after her. "Grandpa," Emily said in a loud, nervous voice. "I'm really sorry that we — uh — used the TASC again without permission."

For a moment Jonathan thought the old man hadn't heard, in spite of the hearing aid in each of his ears. Then Mr. Kenny turned and glared at Emily from under his baseball cap. "Oh, you're sorry for that, are you?" He snorted. "What about breaking your solemn promise to me that you'd never use the TASC again, after the *Titanic*? Are you sorry about that, too?"

Matt and Jonathan stepped around the clutter of cartons and machines waiting for repair to stand beside Emily. "That's not *exactly* what we promised," Matt began in a soothing voice. "We only said — "

"Hmph." The old man pushed his glasses up on his nose with a jab of his forefinger. "Don't come to me with your weasel words. Going to be a politician, are you, Matt? You should be ashamed of yourself. You knew good and well what I *thought* you meant."

Jonathan's face felt warm, and he noticed Matt's turning pink, too. It was true — they might as well have lied, when they promised Mr. Kenny they wouldn't try to go back to the *Titanic*. At that time, the old man thought the TASC couldn't send them to any other destination in time and space.

"I ought to disown you!" Mr. Kenny was getting more worked up, pointing a screwdriver at them with a shaking, gnarled hand. "The three of you!"

Strangely, this last outburst made Jonathan feel a little better. If the old man was talking about *disowning* the three of them, didn't that mean he thought he *owned* the three of them in the first place? At least Mr. Kenny hadn't decided that Matt and Emily were great-grandchildren he was stuck with, but Jonathan was an unrelated young jerk he could get rid of.

But Jonathan's relief faded away as he focused on Mr. Kenny's face. His loose, leathery skin was drawn up in folds of worry. He was more upset than angry, Jonathan realized.

"Time travel is too darned dangerous!" the old man was saying. "It's not worth the risk. Not for the kind of joyriding you were doing."

"But it wasn't joyriding," protested Emily. "Grandpa, we *had* to go see for ourselves how the Revolution really began, what the people were really like, why — "

"Horse manure!" Mr. Kenny said rudely. "You wanted to go for a little joyride. Now, going to the *Titanic*, that was different. You were trying to do somebody else some good. I'd have understood — not approved, mind you, but understood — if you'd gone off on another mission like that. Say, to keep President Lincoln from getting shot."

"Lincoln," Matt said respectfully. He put on his earnest, interested expression, the one that made adults like and trust him. "Would you say he was the best president the country ever had?"

"Darned right," growled the old man. "If Lincoln hadn't been president during the Civil War, the country would have split right in two. We'd be living in the dinky little Northern States of America right now. And who else would have had the guts to free the slaves?"

"Yeah, what a hero," said Matt eagerly. "And isn't it amazing that Abraham Lincoln was like you in a lot of ways? I mean, he educated himself, just like you, Grandpa. And his mother died

7

when he was young, like yours. And he was interested in machines and inventions, like you, right?"

Mr. Kenny shot Matt a suspicious look through his glasses. "Don't try to butter me up. And don't try to get me off the track. Where was I? I was saying, if you kids were trying to do something that would benefit a lot of people, like stop Booth from shooting President Lincoln — But of course you can't change the past."

"Oh, yes, you — " Emily began to exclaim. Then she caught herself and changed her exclamation into a big sneeze. "Dusty in here," she explained.

"Just what I was going to say," agreed her great-grandfather. "Time for spring cleaning. Now, about you three young crooks. What're you going to do to make it up to me?"

"We'll do *anything!*" exclaimed Emily.

"Yeah, yeah," agreed Jonathan and Matt.

But Emily wasn't so enthusiastic when her great-grandfather put a broom in her hands. "We're going to clean up the workshop, like you suggested," he announced. "You boys move the boxes and machines out of Emily's way. Meanwhile, I'll sort out the rubbish. Tomorrow's garbage day, so now's the time to get the trash out to the curb."

This was not the kind of work any of the kids enjoyed, but they didn't dare complain. They spent the next two hours sweeping and lifting and lugging junk to the end of Mr. Kenny's driveway. As Jonathan labored, he kept glancing around the workshop. He couldn't ask, of course, but he very much wanted to know: where was the TASC?

The Time and Space Connector should be hard to miss. It was a clumsy-looking invention, as big as a barbecue grill, fastened on the shelves of a metal cart. Mr. Kenny used to keep the TASC hidden by a gray grill cover, but Jonathan didn't see that, either.

Actually, he thought he did spot the metal cart that had formed the framework for the TASC, over there under the garage window. But where were the projector and clocks and batteries and all the other equipment, connected by a tangle of wires and cables? The shelves of the cart held only a few toasters and other small appliances, tagged and waiting for repair.

"Here, son, these cartons go out." Mr. Kenny motioned Jonathan to a back corner of the workshop.

The three cartons, well sealed with package tape, were large and fairly heavy. Jonathan carried them out to the curb one at a time. As he set the first carton down beside the moldy lawn-chair cushions and a rusty coil of wire, he noticed the black letters on the top: DANGER.

A wild hope burst into Jonathan's mind. Three

9

big, heavy cartons. The three shelves of the TASC stand. His heart started tripping, and he hurried back into the workshop.

"What's in the boxes?" Jonathan asked Mr. Kenny, trying to keep his tone of voice casual.

"What? Oh, the cartons. This and that," the old man said blandly. "Just some odds and ends. I was worried kids might get into them and hurt themselves."

Jonathan nodded without answering, as if he weren't that interested. But inside, he was shouting. I *bet* you were worried about kids getting into this stuff! Kids like me and Matt and Emily! Kids who might go off on another time-travel adventure!

Jonathan didn't question Mr. Kenny any more about the cartons. He carried the second and third cartons out to the curb and went on to the next task. But he felt breathless and light-headed. The Time and Space Connector, all neatly packaged and sitting at the curb, ready for someone to carry home and put back together and go — Jonathan took a deep breath, trying to calm himself.

Finally the workshop was cleaned and tidied to Mr. Kenny's satisfaction. The three kids walked off down the driveway, hot and grimy from their work but feeling much better. As they reached the sidewalk, Jonathan nodded toward the junk at the curb. "Want to bet what's in those three boxes?"

Emily gave him a puzzled look. "The ones that say DANGER? You already asked Grandpa Frank. He said — "

"I know what he *said*," Jonathan interrupted. " 'Kids might get into them, and hurt themselves.' That was his idea of a good joke. Paying us back for pretending to promise him we wouldn't use the TASC again."

Matt frowned down at the DANGER-labeled boxes, then up at his friend. His eyes widened. "The TASC, in those boxes? No! He wouldn't just throw it away, his own invention."

"Yes, he would!" cried Emily. "Let's take the boxes home and see." She stooped to pick up a carton, then looked over her shoulder at the open workshop. Mr. Kenny was standing at his workbench, but he had turned to watch them.

"Keep walking!" whispered Jonathan. "Don't let him think we've noticed the boxes." Emily gave her great-grandfather a big smile and a wave, and walked on.

When they were out of sight of the workshop, Matt said, "We'll have to come back after dark somehow."

"No, we don't have to wait that long," said Emily eagerly. "Grandpa Frank always eats dinner early, like at five-thirty. He won't be watching the sidewalk then."

11

Jonathan shook his head. "No. We can't just take the boxes — Mr. Kenny might look out after dinner and notice they were gone. He'd have a good idea it was us."

The kids had reached the center of town by now. They cut behind the supermarket, heading for the development where Matt and Emily lived.

"So, what do we do?" Matt frowned at the row of Dumpsters behind the supermarket, as if they held the answer. "If we sneak back in the middle of the night, with our luck, some cops will notice us carrying the cartons home."

"We could come back at sunrise," suggested Jonathan. "Except — the trash pickup might get there before us." He pictured the sanitation crew tossing the TASC boxes into their truck, and he felt sick.

"You guys!" exclaimed Emily. She was pointing to the Dumpsters, piled high with empty cartons. For a moment, Jonathan couldn't figure out why she was so excited.

2.
Nothing Dangerous, This Time

The Dumpsters behind the supermarket had a great selection of cartons. It was easy to find three of the same size as the ones at Mr. Kenny's curb. The kids also found plenty of brownish heads of lettuce and rotten potatoes to fill their cartons. "Our substitute boxes have to be heavy, too," Jonathan explained. "Mr. Kenny wouldn't try to lift them, but he just might go out and poke one with his cane, if he gets suspicious."

"Yuck," said Matt. "These boxes are going to stink."

"Not if we seal them up tight," said Emily.

Luckily they had enough money with them to buy a roll of package tape and a black felt marker. By the time they'd taped down the flaps of the cartons and printed DANGER on each one, it was time to sneak back to the old man's house.

A few minutes later, they left Mr. Kenny's

neighborhood at a staggering run, each of them clutching a different carton from the one they'd dropped at the curb. "Wah-hoo!" shouted Matt. "We got it!"

"Yay, TASC!" Emily's face glowed over the top of her carton. "This time, we're setting it up in *my* room."

"No, we'd better take it to my house," said Jonathan. "We can't let your parents see the TASC."

When they thought about it, Matt and Emily had to admit he was right. Of course Mr. and Mrs. Cowen had no idea that the old man's invention actually *worked,* or that their own kids had used it — twice. But they did know that the TASC was supposed to be in Mr. Kenny's workshop, not in Matt's or Emily's room.

As Jonathan and Matt and Emily lugged the heavy cartons through the center of town and uphill along the park overlooking the river, they grew quiet. Finally Emily said, "I just had a horrible thought. I keep smelling rotten vegetables. What if I picked up one of *your* boxes by mistake?"

Jonathan groaned. "I smell it, too. What if we *all* picked up the wrong boxes? We were kind of scrambling there at the curb."

"That's ridiculous," said Matt, but he looked worried. He set his carton down on a park bench and sniffed his fingers. "The smell's on our own

14

hands, you doofuses, from picking up the vegetables."

But now they had to check for sure. Jonathan tore the brown tape from his carton until he could pull up one of the flaps.

From the top of the carton, pink light flashed out at them like a signal. They sighed with relief. *"Yes!"* Emily exclaimed. "The crystal!"

Jonathan grinned. "It sure isn't a rotten potato." The crystal was the rose quartz that fastened over the lens of the TASC projector and guided the resonation between the present and the past. And in the top of Emily's carton they found the destination clock of the TASC, still set for 1775. And under the flaps of Matt's carton, the lid of the blender.

Satisfied, the three kids trudged on up to the apartment building where Jonathan lived with his mother and older sister, Grace. In the Schultzes' apartment they found Grace lounging on the sofa with the TV remote control balanced on one knee. "Hi, couch potato," Jonathan greeted her.

Grace squinted at the cartons. "What's all that stuff? Don't you have enough junk in your room already? And 'DANGER'? What does that mean, explosives?"

"Right," Jonathan told her. "You'd better evacuate the building — maybe for a couple of *years*."

Snickering, the three kids carried the boxes down the hall and into Jonathan's room. His iguana watched them from its cage on top of the bookshelf as they set down the heavy cartons.

"Whew!" Emily said. "I thought my arms were going to drop off. It must be two miles from Grandpa Frank's to Jonathan's."

Matt was shaking out his arms, too, but he looked worried. "Listen, you guys. I think we got carried away. We don't really have any right to the TASC."

"Sure we do," said Jonathan. "Mr. Kenny threw it away."

"So it's not his anymore," Emily added. "Now it belongs to us. And we can do anything we want with it."

"No, we can't." Matt folded his arms, and his deep-set eyes took on a righteous look. "You heard what Grandpa Frank said. He was afraid we were going to get hurt. He said it wasn't worth it."

"So, nothing dangerous, this time." Jonathan spread his arms, accidentally knocking over the birthday card beside his computer. Setting up the card again, he felt a guilty twinge. Mr. Kenny had given him that birthday card. Mr. Kenny treated him like a grandson. Now Jonathan had stolen Mr. Kenny's Time and Space Connector so he could have another adventure

16

with it — just what the old man *didn't* want them to do.

"No, Matt," Emily answered her brother. "Grandpa Frank didn't say time travel wasn't worth it. He said it wasn't worth it unless you were trying to do something to help other people."

Matt didn't answer right away. A faraway look came into his blue-gray eyes. "Something like saving President Lincoln from getting shot," he said softly. Then he shook his head. "It's no use." He looked from Emily to Jonathan. "See, the kind of mission that would help a lot of people is exactly the kind we can't do — because we can't change the past."

"But I found out that we *did*," exclaimed Emily.

"She's right!" Jonathan felt suddenly short of breath. "Your handkerchief in that painting, remember?"

Giving his friend an amazed stare, Matt plopped down on the bed. "*You* said that didn't prove anything. And a handkerchief isn't much of a change, even if it was mine."

Jonathan waved a hand. "Yeah, what Emily saw isn't actually proof, but it's a strong indication. And yeah, a handkerchief isn't that big a change — but we weren't *trying* to change anything in the Revolution."

"Come on, Matt, admit it." Emily sat on the bed beside her brother. "Grandpa Frank would definitely approve of saving Abraham Lincoln."

Matt didn't actually give in. But as the three kids argued, Jonathan thought he could see an adventure-loving gleam appear in his friend's eye. Finally Emily said, "Listen, Matt, why doesn't Jonathan go ahead and see if he can put the TASC together? We haven't really checked the cartons — maybe there's some important piece missing."

"That's true," Jonathan agreed. "And then all this arguing would be for nothing."

"So let him *try* to get it to work again," Emily went on, "while we put together the costumes and stuff for President Lincoln's time." She smiled a big winning smile at her brother. "Then, we promise, if you still say no, we won't try to use the TASC."

When Matt agreed to this, Jonathan was sure they'd won. Once the TASC was up and running, how could Matt refuse a new adventure?

All that evening, Jonathan worked on assembling the Time and Space Connector. The parts were in better shape than he'd feared — he supposed Mr. Kenny couldn't bring himself to throw his precious invention into the cartons like junk. The delicate pieces were wrapped in newspaper, and the spaces in the cartons were filled with Styrofoam beads.

Taking the books and tapes out of his bookcase and moving the iguana to the top of the computer, Jonathan used the three shelves of the bookcase more or less the way Mr. Kenny had originally used the metal cart for the TASC. The projector with the rose quartz fastened over its lens sat on the top shelf. The clocks, one for the present and one for their destination in the past, fit on the middle shelf, along with the batteries and the location finder. And on the bottom shelf went the blender with its electrodes, adapted to provide cold-fusion power.

There was no way to hurry this tedious work. Jonathan measured and fitted and bolted and wired and tested. Hours went by. At some point, his mother made him come out and eat dinner. Late that night, he fell into bed exhausted, with the TASC only half assembled.

The next day was Saturday. Jonathan meant to get up early and make more progress on the TASC before he was due at Mr. Kenny's workshop. But he woke just in time to gulp down juice and a bagel with cream cheese and ride his bike to the old man's neighborhood. Usually, helping Mr. Kenny in his workshop was one of the high points of Jonathan's week. Today he only wanted to stay home and work on the TASC,

19

but he couldn't do anything to make the old man suspicious.

Morning sun shone into Mr. Kenny's garage through the open door, and the old man puttered around the workshop with his cane. "I heard them picking up the trash bright and early this morning," he remarked, eyes twinkling behind his glasses. "Yep, sure was good to get all that rubbish out of my shop." Jonathan said nothing, trying to look politely puzzled. The old man chuckled again.

Early in the afternoon, Matt and Emily walked up Mr. Kenny's driveway. As Emily chatted with the old man, Matt stooped down to watch Jonathan replace the fan belt in a vacuum cleaner.

"We're ready," Matt whispered. "Emily got our outfits. She was in that play, *Tom Sawyer*, last week, so she borrowed three of those costumes. And I've been studying up on Washington in 1865, and planning our missions."

"So, I guess that means you changed your mind," said Jonathan.

"Yeah," admitted Matt. "I mean, the chance to save President Lincoln . . ."

"Did you find a picture for the TASC?" asked Jonathan. The projector needed a photograph of the place they intended to visit, so the TASC could reassemble their molecules at exactly the right spot in time and space.

"Yeah, I got a great picture." Matt glanced across the workshop at his great-grandfather. Mr. Kenny's back was turned. "How about the you-know-what — is it ready?"

"Not yet," Jonathan whispered back. At Matt's disappointed look, he added, "It's not exactly like fixing this vacuum cleaner, you know! For starters, there are over a hundred wires to connect. But I'll probably have it done by tomorrow morning."

After dinner that evening, Jonathan spent the rest of the night working on the TASC again. But just as he thought the Time and Space Connector was ready to go, he remembered the one part that didn't belong on any of the three shelves: the remote control. It was missing.

Jonathan checked all the cartons, although he knew perfectly well they were empty. He searched the carpet inch by inch, although he knew he'd already used every single part. The remote control really was missing. Had Mr. Kenny destroyed that one part, just to make sure that no one could use his invention again? Just in case somebody stole the cartons and reassembled the TASC?

There was only one way around it: Jonathan would have to build a new remote control from scratch. His heart sank.

But wait, Mr. Kenny's remote for the TASC

21

had been just a modified TV remote. Jonathan thought he even remembered the brand name on the casing — wasn't it the same as the Schultzes' TV remote?

Slipping out of his room, Jonathan studied his sister. Grace was (where else?) on the sofa in front of the TV. He'd have to let it go for now, and get up early tomorrow.

The next morning at six, Mrs. Schultz and Grace were sound asleep. Jonathan found the remote control on the living-room floor, next to an empty popcorn bowl. He tiptoed back to his room with the precious item, locked the door, and got to work. By eight-thirty, he had a new control for the TASC. At least, he hoped he did.

After his mother left for church, Jonathan called Matt. "Come as soon as you can," he told him. "We've got to do this before Grace gets up."

"We're on our way," said Matt. "Did you set the TASC for April fourteen, 1865? And eleven-thirty A.M. — that should be about right."

A short while later, Jonathan spotted Matt and Emily riding their bikes down his street, teetering from the weight of their bulging book bags. Jonathan scrambled out of the apartment and down the stairs, to catch them before they rang the bell. "Keep it quiet," he whispered as they came into the apartment. "We can't wake up Grace." He explained about having to use the TV remote.

In Jonathan's room, Emily stared admiringly at the newly assembled TASC on the bookcase. "You did it! Jonathan, you are such a genius."

"Yeah, Schultz, you genius." Matt gave Jonathan a friendly shove. Setting down his book bag, he pulled out a library book. "Look, here's the picture."

Matt showed them a photo of a three-story brick building on an unpaved street. The ground floor was fronted by a row of arches, and rows of arched windows marked the second and third stories. "Ford's Theater, where Booth shot Lincoln on the night of April 14, 1865," said Matt. "Emily's going there on her mission, and the White House is only a few blocks away, so it looked like a good place to land."

"I'm doing the theater part," Emily explained to Jonathan, "because I've been in plays, like *Tom Sawyer.*"

"You aren't going to try to stop John Wilkes Booth, are you?" Jonathan asked in alarm.

"Not by herself — she's just going to show someone else what he's doing, to get him arrested. If that doesn't work, she can still run onto the stage at the last minute and yell at Lincoln to watch out."

"You were going to show me a picture of Booth," Emily reminded her brother.

"Right." Matt turned to another photograph in his book.

Jonathan peered over Emily's shoulder at the young man leaning casually on a railing. His hat was tipped jauntily, shading one side of his handsome face. He held a walking stick in one hand, gloves in the other.

"I'm not sure I can recognize him from that," remarked Emily.

"Yeah, the picture isn't that clear," said Matt. "But you can ask someone else. He was a famous actor, and people at the theater will know him."

Staring at the grainy photograph, Jonathan thought that Booth didn't *look* like a killer. But it was historical fact: Booth had shot an unarmed man — President Lincoln — in the back of the head.

Matt was explaining Jonathan's mission. First, he should try to get an interview with Lincoln himself.

"With the president of the United States? A kid like me?" Jonathan asked doubtfully.

"I know, but Lincoln was a pretty casual guy and he saw visitors all the time," said Matt. "Anyway, if you *do* get in to see President Lincoln, just tell him the truth. Lincoln liked inventions, so explain to him about the TASC. When he's convinced you're from the future, tell him you know that this actor is plotting to kill him at the theater tonight."

As Matt talked, Emily pulled the costumes out of her book bag. She held pantaloons and a frilly dress up to herself, looked in Jonathan's mirror, and made a horrible face. "What are *you* going to do?" she asked her brother.

"I'm going to try to talk to Mrs. Lincoln," said Matt. "It was her idea to go to the theater in the first place. If she changed her mind, they wouldn't go, and Lincoln wouldn't get shot."

"Listen!" Jonathan put up a hand. "Water running in the shower. My sister's up. In a little while, she'll be tearing through the apartment in search of the TV remote."

"Then we'd better put our costumes on and get going." Emily held out clothes to her brother and Jonathan.

As Jonathan dressed, he couldn't help thinking that the worst part of time travel was the geeky costumes you needed to wear. For their last trip, to the American Revolution, he'd actually had to wear a wig. Now he pulled on a white dress shirt, a short jacket with no lapels and a row of buttons, and shapeless, too-short pants with suspenders.

But the clothes Matt had to put on were even worse. Chuckling, Jonathan pointed to Matt's frayed pants and ragged shirt.

"Don't say anything," growled Matt.

There was a knock on the door of Jonathan's

room. "Jonathan?" It was Grace's voice. "Have you seen the remote?"

Jonathan, turning on the projector of the TASC, had just realized that they didn't have a screen. He had to cover up his plaid wallpaper with something white. Frantically, he started pulling lengths of computer paper out of his printer. He answered his sister in what he hoped was an innocent voice. "Weren't you using it last night?"

That ought to hold Grace for a while. Jonathan motioned to Matt and Emily to help him tape the paper screen up on the wall. He made chalk marks on the carpet between the projector and the screen.

"Here we go!" Emily's voice rose with excitement as she stared at the blown-up photograph on the screen, pink because of the crystal in front of the projector lens. The arched entrances to Ford's Theater looked dark and mysterious.

"Jonathan." Grace was outside the locked door again, and now her voice was suspicious. "I looked all around. You've got it in there, haven't you? What are you doing?"

"Hurry," Emily whispered, tying the ribbons of her bonnet. She and Matt stood on their chalk marks. Their shadows stood on the street in front of Ford's Theater.

"Just a minute," said Matt, plucking his one suspender. "We need a time and place to check in with each other. Let's say three o'clock, at the Washington Monument. You can see it from anywhere in the city."

"Yeah, fine," Jonathan whispered. "Let's go! My sister knows how to pick that lock." Stepping into place, he faced the pink light of the TASC projector.

"Jonathan! I'm opening this door." There was a fiddling, clicking noise.

"Ready for TRANSPORT." Jonathan raised the TASC control and pointed it toward the resonator unit. *"Don't move!"* He pressed the button.

"Just wait till Mom gets home," Grace went on. The doorknob turned. "You're going to be . . ."

As Grace's voice faded away, Jonathan had time to wonder how well his makeshift remote for the TASC would work. He thought he'd guessed how Mr. Kenny had configured the TASC control, but maybe he was wrong. If the three of them ended up permanently stuck in hyperspace, it would be his fault.

And then Jonathan felt himself dissolve. This is normal for time travel, he told himself to keep down his panic. In time travel, it was normal to feel your molecules rushing through hyperspace, like electromagnetic waves beamed from a transmitter toward a television screen. But it made Jonathan want to scream his lungs out.

3.
"Call Me Hamlet"

Emily, all the little bits of her, whooshed through hyperspace. She loved the adventures, but she'd always hated the actual time-travel part. Somehow, it was much more terrifying than any of the other scary things that had happened to her.

On their first time-travel adventure, Emily had barely escaped from a sinking ship. On the second, she'd run through a battlefield, dodging British musket balls. But this dissolving-molecules feeling was the scariest — as if there were no more to Emily Ann Cowen than a Kool-Aid tablet dropped into water.

Then Emily felt solid ground under her feet — solid, but bumpy. She stumbled and fell on her knees. She would have skinned them if she hadn't been wearing a dress and petticoats and those ridiculous pantaloons.

Looking up, Emily saw Jonathan and Matt

lunging away from her, toward the other side of the street. "Watch out, Emily!" Matt yelled over his shoulder.

Hooves clopped, wheels squeaked. Two horses were pulling a carriage straight toward her. The driver saw Emily. He was shouting, trying to turn the horses. Emily jumped up, but she stepped on the hem of her dress, ripping it. She fell on her knees again.

Emily knew exactly what to do next: throw herself to one side, rolling out of the way. But she couldn't do it. It was like one of those crunch moments in a softball game, when time seems to stretch out. You can see perfectly well what you want your arms and legs to do, except they're moving in slow motion. And you know they won't make it.

Then someone grabbed Emily under the arms, yanking her out of the path of the carriage. It rolled by so close that Emily could have counted the spokes on the iron-rimmed wheels.

"My, that was close!" said a mellow voice above her. "Are you hurt, dear?"

Set on her feet on the wooden sidewalk, Emily turned to see a young man in a dark suit and light overcoat gazing down at her. He was pale, with dark, liquid eyes and a silky black mustache. As handsome as a movie star, thought Emily. She almost felt that she'd actually seen him in a movie, although of course she couldn't have because they didn't make movies back then.

"Didn't you notice the carriage coming?" he asked. He looked as worried for her as Dad had been, the time Emily fell off the garage roof. Behind him was a cluster of curious faces, and a babble of comments: " — doctor? — driving quite recklessly, and the police — girls ought to be home, where — "

"I'm fine," Emily said in an almost-firm voice. Now that she was safe, she had time to be mad that they hadn't planned things better. They'd been so stupid, choosing a *street* for the landing site! The street in front of Ford's Theater had been empty in the photograph, but of course carriages and wagons must drive back and forth here all the time. "I fell down, and *then* I saw the carriage, but — "

"There, don't try to talk." The young man gave a wave of dismissal to the people gathered around them. Guiding Emily toward the steps of the theater, he gathered up his hat, gloves, walking stick, and some letters. "Come in, sit and rest a while. I'll have one of the ladies help you to tidy up." With a hand on Emily's shoulder, he ushered her through one of the archways and into the theater.

Yes! Emily grinned to herself. Almost being run over was turning out to be wonderful luck.

She wondered what kind of story she could make up to get them to let her hang around Ford's Theater. And she *had* to stay, because it was here that Emily would have her chance to expose John Wilkes Booth as an assassin.

Booth was supposed to show up at the theater sometime in the afternoon. The idea was for Emily to keep an eye on him until he sneaked upstairs and started setting up the president's theater box for the murder. He'd drill a spy hole in the inside door of the box and leave a piece of wood handy to jam the outside door. If Emily could get somebody else, like the theater manager, to see what Booth was doing, the assassin would be arrested. And President Lincoln would be saved.

Now she had a good excuse to be in Ford's Theater, *and* she had a guide. From the way he talked, this young man must have some connection with the theater. Emily smiled up at her rescuer.

"That's the style. Brave girl!" He beamed at Emily as they walked down the center aisle.

Emily gazed up at the stage, where some actors were rehearsing a scene. She sniffed the paint and lumber smells of the sets, which seemed to suggest an elegant house. Emily wished *she* could be up there rehearsing, too. *Tom Sawyer* had been a lot of fun, and she was sorry it was over.

Emily's new friend led her up the steps to the stage as if he had a perfect right to be there, and the rehearsing actors paid them no attention. "Are you an actor?" whispered Emily when they were in the wings.

"Yes, but not in this production," said the young man. "You don't know who I am?" He smiled teasingly. "Allow me to introduce myself. You may call me — " He paused, and a very different expression came over his face.

As though somebody he loved had died, thought Emily.

"Call me Hamlet," he finished in a low, intense tone. There was a pause, and then he smiled at her again. "And you? Surely I've seen this winsome face and Titian ringlets behind the footlights?"

Whoa, what flattery, she thought. "I'm Emily Cowen. Actually I *was* in a play, just last week. *Tom Sawyer.* I only had a little part, but I liked it."

"Don't know *Tom Sawyer*," said the young man gallantly "but I'm sure you were an ornament to the production. Now, let's see about finding you a drink of water. Miss Gourlay generally keeps a pitcher on her dressing table."

"Uh — I don't think I want any water, after all." Emily had just remembered Matt's warning about the water in Washington, D.C., in

32

1865. "It has sewage in it," he'd told her. "Don't drink it unless it's boiled! You'll get something horrible, like typhoid fever."

"Hamlet" seemed determined to give Emily *something* to drink. Disappearing up the back-stage stairs for a few moments, he reappeared with a cup of tea and a cookie. After Emily had finished her refreshments, they went out to the front of the theater and sat down to watch the rehearsal.

"You don't mind waiting for a bit, do you?" asked the actor. "As soon as Miss Laura Keene is through rehearsing, I'll ask her to have some-one mend your dress."

Of course Emily didn't mind, as long as she could stay in the theater. Anyway, it was fun to sit here chatting and watching the actors. They were really hamming it up — striding back and forth, flinging their arms out in dramatic ges-tures, tossing their heads.

Every time the young man smiled down at Emily, she felt his charm like a heat lamp. She'd never met anyone this good-looking and charm-ing. In fact, at first she wondered, suspiciously, why he would bother charming *her*. But after a while she decided he must just be the kind of person who walked around all the time with his CHARM switch on. She thought of Jonathan's older sister, Grace, who was always in love with some rock star. If Grace ever met this guy, and he looked at her with those melting eyes, she would probably faint.

"What abominable overacting!" Waving a hand at the stage, the young man winked at Emily. "But *Our American Cousin* is that kind of play. It's a huge success, but for half the money I'd rather play Shakespeare, any time. *Macbeth. King Lear. Julius Caesar . . . Hamlet.*"

Gazing off into the shadowy theater, the actor went on in a darker tone. "But the most tragic drama of all has been played out on the stage of the nation." A desperate look came into his brilliant dark eyes. "Oh, little Emily, it was a noble cause, it was the cause of Beauty and Freedom. It was a glorious dream. Now — now, my beloved fatherland lies bleeding and broken. We are slaves of the ape-king tyrant."

Emily watched "Hamlet" uneasily. What in the world was he talking about? "I thought the slaves were free now."

He didn't seem to hear her. "And what have *I* done, while that noble band of patriotic heroes gave their lives, battling tyranny?" With a thump of his fist on his chest, he spoke what sounded like lines from a play:

"I, the son of a dear father murdered,
    Prompted to my revenge . . ."

With a bitter laugh, "Hamlet" added in a low tone, "I have done *nothing*." He clasped his walking stick as if it were a sword hilt.

An idea half-formed itself in Emily's mind. She almost knew who this man sitting next to her was. But before the idea came clear, two men started down the stairs from the stage. One of them was well dressed, wearing a suit with a silver watch chain across his vest. As they walked up the aisle, he was giving instructions to the other man, a workman in a collarless dark shirt.

"First, Ed," said the man in the suit, "take the partition out of that box." He pointed up to the box, hung with lace and gold satin draperies and lined with red wallpaper, at the right of the stage.

"Yessir, Mr. Ford," said Ed.

"And then bring that red rocking chair down from upstairs — you know the one I mean," Mr. Ford went on. "President Lincoln likes a rocker." Catching sight of the man beside Emily, he waved and grinned. "Hello, there, Booth!"

Booth. Emily gasped and stared at "Hamlet." Of course she'd seen him before — in Matt's library book!

"Are you John Wilkes Booth?" she demanded.

He gave her an amused look, as if everybody in the world, except Emily, knew who he was.

Then he raised a hand to Mr. Ford. "What's the news, Harry?"

Harry Ford paused with his hands in his jacket pockets, his eyes twinkling. "I've got some *fine* news for you. You see, your good friends, President and Mrs. Lincoln, are attending tonight's performance."

At these words, Booth's handsome face twisted, twitching with rage. Like a monster in a horror movie, thought Emily, shrinking back. If she'd seen him like that before, she never would have called him good-looking.

Booth leaped out of his chair, shoving it into the row behind with a clatter.

With a look of alarm, Ed scurried off toward the lobby. Ford, backing down the aisle, put up his hands. "Only a joke, John."

The grimace faded from Booth's face, but he didn't smile. He pushed his silk hat onto his head and tucked his walking stick under one arm. In a voice so low that Emily could barely hear him, he muttered,

"O, from this time forth,
My thoughts be bloody, or be nothing worth!"

Then John Wilkes Booth strode up the aisle and out of the theater.

4.
Bloody Thoughts

"*Whew!*" Harry Ford stared after Booth. "I'm glad this war is over. It's as much as your life is worth to make a joke." His glance fell on Emily. "And who are you, little miss?"

Emily introduced herself and explained about almost getting run over, and Mr. Booth rescuing her.

"But surely you have someone nearby — your mother, your father, perhaps an aunt?"

"Not really," Emily said cautiously. She and Matt had talked about how she would explain why she was hanging around Ford's Theater all by herself. They had decided the best excuse was that she loved plays and hoped she'd get a chance to be in one. Now Emily wondered if something connected with her near-accident in the street wouldn't be a better excuse.

Fortunately, Mr. Ford didn't seem to be paying close attention to Emily. He was gazing down the aisle to the stage, where a woman with auburn ringlets and a commanding way of carrying herself was giving directions for tonight's performance. Although the woman's voice was high and sweet, with a British accent, her tone of voice and forceful gestures reminded Emily of her softball coach: *This* is what went wrong last night. *This* is how you're going to do it tonight. *No* excuses. Go for it!

Now she was speaking over the footlights to a man placing sheet music on the music stands. "As you know, President and Mrs. Lincoln are attending tonight's performance."

"And General and Mrs. Grant, too, Miss Keene," Harry Ford called up to the stage.

Miss Keene smiled. "All the better! The hero of the hour, attending our very last performance — *that* will run up box-office receipts. Are you putting out notices about the Grants, Mr. Ford? Good." She turned back to the musician. "Now, when the Lincolns and the Grants appear in their box, I will signal, thus." She waved dramatically at the gold-curtained box to her left. "And you will strike up 'Hail to the Chief.' Is that understood?"

Not waiting for an answer, Laura Keene turned from the orchestra leader and fixed her sharp gaze on Emily. With a ladylike but purposeful stride she came down the steps from the stage, her full skirts swaying. "Harry, who is this?"

38

Emily stood up and curtsied, as if she were acting her part in *Tom Sawyer*.

"She says her name is Emily," said Harry Ford. "It seems that Booth saved her from being run over by a carriage and brought her in here to rest."

Looking thoughtful, Miss Keene stretched out her hand to lift a lock of Emily's red curls. "This is just the charming, lively face I had in mind to add interest to the play. Where are your mama and papa, dear?"

Yes, use the accident, thought Emily. Putting her hand to her forehead as if it hurt, she closed her eyes and gave a little moan. "I — I don't think anyone I know is nearby. Right before I saw the carriage coming toward me, all I remember is falling through space." That was the absolute truth, and she didn't have to pretend a shudder. "It was the worst feeling I've ever had."

Laura Keene was watching Emily with a raised eyebrow, the corners of her mouth twitching. Emily felt foolish — of course this woman of the theater would know that Emily was putting on an act. Then Miss Keene gave Emily a sudden brilliant smile, and Emily smiled back hopefully.

"And you have fine teeth, too, my dear," said Miss Keene. "Such an advantage on the stage."

"Laura," Harry Ford broke in, "This little girl is not well. Can't she go backstage and lie down?

Perhaps the fright has stunned her mind."

"Or perhaps she is stagestruck," Miss Keene murmured with a little laugh. But she took Emily by the hand and led her backstage and up the stairs, into her own dressing room. There she hung up Emily's bonnet and let her lie down on a cot behind a screen. Emily heard Miss Keene talking to the costume woman about the "peculiar" clothes Emily was wearing. "So old-fashioned, yet they seem quite newly made."

Then Miss Keene went away, and Emily lay on the cot wondering what to do now. She was in the theater, but this wasn't a good place to wait for John Wilkes Booth to return and set up the presidential box for Lincoln's assassination. Booth could come and go and Emily would never know it, if she had to stay backstage.

After a while a servant brought her a bowl of broth and a roll, which Emily tried to sip and nibble as if she weren't feeling well. The way she actually felt was starved. She and Matt had been in such a hurry this morning, after Jonathan's call, that she'd eaten only a little bowl of Cheerios.

Just as Emily was sitting on the edge of the cot, thinking about sneaking out and hiding upstairs in the balcony, Laura Keene returned. She glanced at the empty bowl and plate, then beamed at Emily. "Are you feeling better, my dear? I'm so glad." She sat beside the cot and took Emily's hand. "Do you remember anything more? No? Never mind; we won't fret just now. I've sent a note to the police station, in case your people come looking for you. In the meantime, you may stay here."

"Maybe I could do something to help, while I'm waiting," suggested Emily.

Laura Keene gave Emily one of her charming smiles. "Do you know, you *might* be able to help us. If you are still here this evening, do you think you might take a very small part in *Our American Cousin*?"

"I would love that," said Emily. "I've been in plays before."

"Ah — I rather thought you had acted," Miss Keene said sweetly. "See here, I've marked the lines where I wish you to come on." She handed Emily a script, and showed her four places where she'd inserted a bit for a "Child."

Leading Emily to the stage, Miss Keene instructed her about where she wanted her to stand and what she wanted her to do. Emily wasn't supposed to say anything at all. She just had to be on stage in a certain place at the right time and act astonished, or indignant, or horrified, or overjoyed.

"First-rate!" said Miss Keene after she'd put Emily through her paces. "That will add a very nice touch. Now the costume woman will fit you with something suitable. And then you may spend the afternoon studying the script, to make sure you know your cues."

After the fitting for her costume, Emily took her script out into the seats in the theater. Things couldn't have worked out better if she and Matt had planned it this way, she thought. Now she had an excuse to be at Ford's Theater all afternoon and evening.

Standing in the middle of the aisle, Emily looked around the empty theater. It was pretty, with its gold-draped boxes, its fluted white pillars supporting the balcony, its carved moldings around the ceiling. But it wasn't very big — no larger than the Newbury High School auditorium where *Tom Sawyer* had been put on. It was funny how you expected that important things could happen only in important-looking places. But President Lincoln had been shot in this little theater, in that little box up there above the stage, sitting in that fuddy-duddy rocking chair.

Settling in the last row of seats, to keep an eye on the theater entrance, Emily began to read. It was perfect, too, that she had a copy of the play, so she could learn exactly where to expect "the funniest line." Matt had told her that was when Booth planned to shoot President Lincoln, because the roars of laughter would cover the gunshot.

Emily remembered the way Booth had looked when he'd talked about his "beloved fatherland."

42

He meant the Confederacy, the South, of course. The Civil War had just ended, and the South — the "cause of Beauty and Freedom," according to Booth — had lost.

Emily didn't see how anyone could feel that way about a country that allowed slavery. It made *her* feel sick. But a lot of people must have agreed with Booth, or there wouldn't have been any Civil War.

But Miss Keene and Mr. Ford didn't seem to be against President Lincoln. If only Booth came back to the theater, the way Matt had predicted! (Matt knew a lot of history, but he wasn't always one hundred percent right about things.) Then Emily could get Miss Keene or Mr. Ford to watch Booth setting up the president's box for the assassination. And then Booth would be arrested this afternoon, long before he had the chance to take aim at the president.

The only problem with that was, then Emily, Matt, and Jonathan would return to their own time. Maybe Emily could talk the boys into staying a few more hours, so that Emily wouldn't have to give up her part in *Our American Cousin*. It would be fun. And in spite of Miss Keene's bossiness, Emily liked her and wanted to show her what a good job she could do.

Just in case, and also because she didn't have anything else to do, Emily read. The play was very old-fashioned, about a British mother trying to marry her daughter off to a rich Yankee who didn't know how to act in polite society. Still, there were places that made Emily giggle, and she knew that plays were always funnier when they were acted out on the stage.

Yawning, Emily squirmed, then lay down on her stomach across the row of chairs. She wished she knew what time it was. Matt had said John Wilkes Booth would come to set up the president's box during the afternoon, but he wasn't sure exactly when.

Emily was getting toward the end of the script, but she hadn't come to the "funniest line" yet. Wait — here it was. The mother who was trying to get the rich Yankee to marry her daughter discovered that he'd given away his money. She lost her temper and accused him of not knowing good manners.

Then the Yankee said, "I guess I know enough to turn you inside out, you sockdologizing old man-trap." *That* was their idea of funny? Please! But she was pretty sure it was the line Matt was talking about.

Then Emily heard a noise that made her raise her head from the script. Somebody had opened the front door of the theater. She could hear creaky footsteps in the lobby. Emily froze.

Emily pressed herself flat against the chair seats. A figure in black passed her row without turning his head. He walked on down the aisle to the orchestra area, where he searched quietly among the music stands.

Then he was gliding back up the aisle with a piece of wood in his hand. That must be the stick that Matt had told Emily about. Tonight, Booth would use it to jam the outer door of the president's box from inside.

In the gloom of the dimly lit theater, Booth's black clothes blended into the dark background. Light from the windows over the balcony seemed to fall only on his white face. Again John Wilkes Booth walked past Emily's row without looking to either side.

Like a sleepwalker. A sleepwalker with bloody thoughts. Emily remembered the last lines that Booth had quoted.

O, from this time forth,
My thoughts be bloody, or be nothing worth!

The actor disappeared into the lobby, but there was no sound of the theater door opening and closing again. Instead, Emily heard soft footsteps climbing the stairs. He's going up to the box, Emily thought.

Emily waited a moment, until the footsteps faded away. Then, slipping off the chairs, she crept into the lobby and up the stairs after him. She wished she were wearing sneakers, instead of these hard-soled party shoes. And it was hard to step quietly, the way her knees were trembling.

Emily didn't scare easily, but she was afraid of the expression on the face she'd just seen floating up the theater aisle. She was afraid of this man who was grieving for the dead Confederacy.

At the top of the stairs Emily tiptoed around the back of the balcony toward a white door. As she neared the door, she heard a quiet crunching and splintering. He must be drilling the peephole in the door to the box.

The outer door was shut. Emily didn't dare open it, but she put her ear to the crack. The drilling stopped for a moment, and Emily heard another noise. It chilled her blood. It was a sort of grunting, rasping breathing. Like some kind of animal.

The drilling started up again. Emily straightened and backed away from the door, quietly, quietly. All she had to do was get someone else to come up here, and they'd see for themselves.

As Emily hurried around the bend of the staircase, she heard a cheerful whistling below. Harry Ford, the theater manager, was crossing the lobby.

"Mr. Ford!" Emily's voice came out in a weird squeak, and the manager looked up, startled. "Please come up!" she went on. "Something terrible — Mr. Booth is setting up — He's going to kill President Lincoln!"

Harry Ford gave her a baffled stare. Then he rushed up the stairs — but he stopped on the landing and seized Emily by the arm. Putting a hand on her forehead, he studied her face. "Are you feverish? I thought Miss Keene had you lie down. Come, you must rest, little girl."

He pulled her through the theater, up to the stage and into the wings. Emily protested, but not too loudly, for fear Booth might hear her.

Backstage, they found Laura Keene giving directions to a stagehand. "Miss Keene," Ford interrupted her, "this child can't be allowed to wander around the theater. She's having delusions. The doctor ought to be sent for."

"Please listen to me, Miss Keene," Emily said desperately. She told how she had seen Booth come into the theater, take a stick from the music stands, and sneak up to the box. She described the sounds she'd heard.

"You ought to be ashamed, young lady," Ford said sharply, "talking this way about Mr. Booth. He saved your life, pulling you from in front of that carriage."

Laura Keene had listened to Emily with a deepening frown. Now she asked, "Did you *see* Mr. Booth drilling a hole in the door?"

"No," admitted Emily. "The outside door of the box was closed, so I couldn't see anything."

Miss Keene looked at Ford and shrugged. "It would do no harm to go look at the box."

Ford grumbled that he had more important things to do, but the three of them went back through the theater and climbed the stairs to the balcony. They tiptoed over to the white door, but now there was no sound from the box.

"I bet he's gone now," Emily said accusingly to Harry Ford.

Sure enough, when Ford opened the outer door, they looked through the empty box to the stage. Emily stared around the box at the little red sofa, at the red-upholstered rocking chair directly in front of the inner door. She pushed past the others and pulled the inner door toward them. She could feel the splintery hole.

"Look! Look at this! I *told* you he drilled a hole. That's so he can peek through and see where the President is, right before he shoots him!"

"Hush," Miss Keene told Emily in an angry tone. "I don't see anything." But she put her hand on the freshly drilled hole. "Harry, have you a match?"

Ford fumbled in his pockets, then struck a match on the sole of his shoe. It flared, and for a few seconds the light flickered over a hole as wide as Laura Keene's forefinger.

"This doesn't prove a thing," Ford said as the match died. "Most likely, Ed poked that hole accidentally when he was taking down the partition here." He gestured at the middle of the box. "Ed's all right, but he does sloppy work if you don't keep an eye on him."

Miss Keene turned toward Emily with a very stern expression, clear to Emily even in the murky light. "Emily. You have allowed your imagination to run away with you. I will not have this." Grasping Emily by the shoulders, she shook her hard. "Nothing shall spoil the triumph of this evening — nothing. Is that understood?"

Emily was shocked, then angry. Nobody ever pushed her around, except in a game where she could push right back. An angry answer to Miss Keene was on the tip of her tongue, but she swallowed it. Chill, she told herself. She forced a nod.

In a gentler voice, Miss Keene went on, "Come, you must lie down and remain quiet until this evening. But if there is another outburst, you may not appear in the play."

The three of them went back downstairs, Emily trailing behind the other two with her fists clenched. She *mustn't* lose her place in the play. It was perfect for the second part of her mission, in case Jonathan's mission and Matt's mission both failed. Then Emily would have to run on-stage, shouting a last-minute warning to President Lincoln.

In front of Emily, Mr. Ford and Miss Keene were talking in low tones. Ford had murmured something about Emily needing a doctor. "Nonsense," answered Miss Keene. "Firmness is all that's wanted with an hysterical imagination. You saw how quickly the child quieted down."

There was a pause, and then Harry Ford remarked, "Wilkes Booth *has* been moody lately, though, hasn't he? And taking too much hard liquor, in my opinion."

"It is a family trait, with him," said Laura Keene, as if that explained everything. "His father, Junius Booth — what a splendid Shakespearean actor *he* was — drank heavily. And he went quite mad at times. They say he flew into such a frenzy, playing Othello, that he actually would have smothered Desdemona on stage. They pulled him away from her only just in time."

"Actors!" snorted Ford. "They can't keep it straight, what's playacting and what's real life." Noticing Miss Keene's cold stare, he cleared his throat. "Present company excepted, I'm sure."

Emily took her script back to Laura Keene's dressing room and lay down on the cot again. Catching sight of the brass clock on the dressing table, she sat up with a gasp. She and Jonathan were supposed to meet Matt at the Washington Monument at three o'clock. It was now almost three-fifteen.

Emily bit her lip. She ought to tell Matt and Jonathan what had happened with her. And she badly wanted to know how they'd done. But if she were caught sneaking out of the theater, Miss Keene might get fed up with Emily and take away her part in the play. If Matt or Jonathan *had* to talk to her, they knew where to find her — at her post.

5.
A Pebble
in Niagara

Even while Jonathan's molecules were still rushing, disassembled, through hyperspace, it dawned on him that they'd picked a dangerous place to land. But his mind was so full of the usual panic of time travel that he couldn't really worry about the next thing until he felt his reassembled feet on solid ground again.

Then Jonathan was staggering on an unpaved street. And sure enough, a horse-drawn carriage was bearing down on them.

Jonathan and Matt leaped in the same direction, to the safety of a wooden sidewalk. "Watch out, Emily!" shouted Matt. And before Jonathan could breathe a sigh of relief, Matt let out another cry. "Where is she?"

Turning, Jonathan saw the carriage rattling past, but no Emily. For an instant he felt sick. Then he pointed across the street. Emily was sprawled on the boards in front of the theater steps. And a man was helping her up.

"*Whew!*" Matt's face, which had been drained of color, started to turn pink. "That was my stupid fault, picking the photo of this street. Well, I guess it turned out okay. Look, that guy's taking her into the theater. Excellent."

The man's back was turned now, as he guided Emily up the steps. But Jonathan had caught a glimpse of his handsome face, the dashing mustache and the dark soulful eyes, and he thought he almost recognized him. Of course he didn't — the only face in 1865 that Jonathan could expect to recognize was Abraham Lincoln's.

"So, Emily's all set." Matt shook his head and wiggled his shoulders, as if he was trying to shake off the scare. "We'd better head on toward the White House." He must have memorized the route, because after a careful look around, Matt led Jonathan down the sidewalk for a block or so.

The day was warm, but the low clouds looked threatening, and Jonathan noticed that the other people on the street were carrying umbrellas. "I wish you'd checked the weather," he grumbled.

Matt shrugged. "If it rains, we get wet; that's all." He pointed to the corner ahead, where a man was selling newspapers. "We turn here — this should be Pennsylvania Avenue." As they turned the corner, he added, "Yeah, because there's the Kirkwood Hotel." Matt craned his neck to read the lettering over the awning. "And there's the *Evening Star* newspaper office, across the street. If we just keep walking up Pennsylvania Avenue, we'll come to the White House."

Remembering how he'd gotten totally lost on the last adventure, Jonathan took a careful look at the landmarks. Pennsylvania Avenue was paved — *that* was a kind of landmark — and there were double lines of tracks down the middle of the street. In fact, there went a streetcar, pulled along the tracks by a team of horses. It parted a throng of horseback riders, carriages, wagons, and people on foot. Jonathan kept thinking that this block must be closed off to traffic, to keep it safe for pedestrians and horse-drawn vehicles. But of course this *was* the traffic — there wasn't any other kind.

The streetcar halted, blocked by a procession that took up most of the avenue. A hundred or so ragged men were being herded along by soldiers in blue uniforms. Jonathan's first impression was that these must be a bunch of homeless people, with their dirty clothes, hollow cheeks, and dazed, weary faces.

Across the street, a man clutching a bottle staggered out of a ramshackle building. "Johnny Reb!" he jeered at the sad parade. "Yah, where's your rebel yell now?"

"The poor guys," said Matt to Jonathan. "You

know who they are? They're southerners, Confederate soldiers, prisoners of war."

"I couldn't even tell they were soldiers," said Jonathan. Their shirts and trousers might once have been gray, but now they were just the color of dirt. They trudged along in boots with flapping soles and toes sticking out.

The boys walked on, past an organ grinder and his audience, past pie shops and shoeshine stands and saloons. "Grover's Theater," said Matt, pointing out a long building topped with an American flag. "Lincoln goes to plays there, too." Posters outside announced the current show: *Aladdin, or, The Magic Lamp.*

"Speaking of Lincoln," began Jonathan.

"Yeah, you lucky guy," Matt interrupted. "Why can't I be the one to meet Lincoln? Never mind," he went on. "I know it has to be you. You're the only one who can explain how the TASC works."

"Don't get too envious," said Jonathan drily. "I might not even get in the door of the White House."

The boys crossed the street, passed a massive marble structure, and rounded another corner. Jonathan caught sight of a familiar white building set back from the street. "Hey, the White House. It looks just the same."

"Yeah — the rest of Washington looks more like some hick town, doesn't it?" Matt paused in front of the iron fence, gazing across the lawn at the White House entrance with its four tall pillars. "Well — good luck."

"Hold on!" exclaimed Jonathan. "I wasn't kidding when I said I might not get to see the president. Then what?"

"I thought I told you," said Matt. "Then you go to the War Department, right next to the White House." He pointed to a brick building farther down the street. "Ask to talk to Stanton; he's the secretary of war. He was paranoid about Confederate plots to kill the president, so I bet he'll listen." Matt lifted a hand in farewell. "See you at three o'clock at the Washington Monument."

Matt walked past the sentries, soldiers standing guard at the iron gates, down the circular drive, and through the gardens toward the back of the White House. But Jonathan paused for a moment outside the gates. Now that he was here, his mission seemed ridiculous. He watched a few people go in past him: men in coats and string ties and hats, women in bonnets and jackets and gloves, with swinging bell-like skirts. Maybe *they* would be let in to see the president, but a sixth-grade kid with too-short pants? Come *on*.

But President Lincoln was going to be shot. *That* wasn't ridiculous. Right now, somewhere in the city, John Wilkes Booth might be loading his pistol to shoot the president of the United States in the back of the head. Jonathan had to give this mission his best, no matter how stupid he felt. He straightened his shoulders and pushed a lock of hair back from his forehead.

As Jonathan walked through the gates, around the drive, and up the steps of the White House, he expected someone to stop him at any minute. Some broad-shouldered Secret Service agent with dark glasses — no, no dark glasses, in 1865 — would grab him by the back of the neck. They'd search him, yell at him, and hustle him back out.

But nobody stopped Jonathan, or any of the people ahead of him. As he climbed the steps, he noticed a uniformed doorman at the front door. He was speaking to each person briefly, then letting him or her in.

"Name and business?" he greeted Jonathan. "If you've come to play with Tad, he just ran around to the back gardens."

"Jonathan Schultz," answered Jonathan stiffly, as if he hadn't "played" with anyone for many years. "I have to see the president. About something very important."

The doorman laughed in a kindly way. "That's what they all say. If it were up to Tom Pendel" — he jerked a thumb toward his chest — "I wouldn't give them the time of day. But President Lincoln listens to everyone. You won't get to see him this morning, though. He's meeting with the Cabinet."

Oh, great, thought Jonathan. Why didn't Matt tell him about this? "But I *have* to see President Lincoln. I could wait."

The doorkeeper laughed again. "Wait? I suppose you *could*." He waved Jonathan in the door. "Around to your right, then, and up the staircase. You'll have plenty of company."

Hurrying up the elegant sweep of the stairs, Jonathan saw that the doorkeeper was right. The long hall at the top of the stairs was almost full. People stood around under the chandelier, singly or in small groups. They paced the hall, leaned against the fancy wallpaper.

There were several doors off the hall, and Jonathan wondered which one led to the president's office. Watching the crowd for a few minutes, he noticed that their eyes kept turning toward one certain door at the far end of the hall. He headed in that direction, brushing by two women. They looked vaguely alike, but one was young, and the other was middle-aged.

As Jonathan worked his way around their hoopskirts, the younger woman said, "Surely the president will pardon Ben, Mother, now that the war is over." Her mother didn't answer, but she linked her arm through her daughter's and squeezed her hand.

Against the wall, a group of men with impassive weathered faces and long black hair stood apart from the rest. They made a few quiet remarks to each other, in a language Jonathan didn't recognize.

The Native Americans were getting some looks of distaste from a group of men in suits and stovepipe hats. "In my opinion," said one of them, "they ought to have a separate waiting room for gentleman applicants for government office. Someone ought to be aware that *I* carry a letter from the assistant to the undersecretary of state." He touched his coat pocket.

"Oh, yes, a dreadful mistake, Dobbins, to make *you* wait with the riffraff!" teased another man. But he also cast a frown at a nearby soldier in a blue Union Army uniform.

Jonathan leaned against the wall next to the soldier, wondering what their problem with him was. The man's brown face was clean-shaven, and his uniform was tidy. You'd think if anyone had a right to see the president, it would be a soldier who'd helped win the war. "Excuse me, sir. I was wondering what you wanted to see President Lincoln about."

The soldier blinked in surprise at the "sir," but he answered, "Well, now, I'm thinking Mr. Lincoln would say I ought to get my pay, if he knowed about it. The major at the Pay Department, he 'splained why he couldn't give it to me. But I jus' think Mr. Lincoln, if he knowed about my wife and my five chil'en I've got to feed, he'd do something for me."

Jonathan wished *he* could do something for the soldier. "Listen, let's make a deal. If I get to see the president first, I'll tell him about your problem. And if you get to see him before I do, will you tell him Jonathan Schultz is out here with an *incredible* invention to show him?"

"An invention, now? Imagine that!" The soldier grinned at the idea, but he shook the hand Jonathan held out. "I surely will tell Mr. Lincoln 'bout your invention. And you tell him Corporal Joshua Brown of the Nineteenth Colored Regiment needs his pay mighty bad."

The corporal fell into a worried silence. Leaning back against the wall, Jonathan wondered how the president *did* decide who to see first. There ought to be numbers you could take, like at a deli counter.

After a long while the well-dressed men left, grumbling and arguing about where to have lunch. Another long while went by. Finally, there was a rustle near the door. "It's the usher!"

As the door opened, all the people in the hall crowded toward that end. A man in a uniform like the doorman's stepped out.

"I wish to convey the president's regrets," the usher said in an important voice. "The Cabinet meeting was unavoidably prolonged, and now the president must go to lunch. If you will return on Monday, he will see you then."

A chorus of groans went up. Instead of leaving, the petitioners crowded in more closely on the usher, explaining in louder and louder voices why *they* should be allowed to see President Lincoln now. Jonathan wiggled his long, thin self through the knot of people. As the usher tried to slip back through the door and close it at the same time, Jonathan grabbed his coattail. "Wait! I've got this completely astounding invention."

The usher turned, trying to brush off Jonathan's hand. "Go along, now. The audience hours are over."

"But I won't be here Monday," pleaded Jonathan. "I'm only in town for today. And I have this invention — President Lincoln loves inventions, right? — that will knock the president's socks off."

The usher tried to keep on frowning, but a laugh sputtered out. "Knock the president's socks off! You're an impudent fellow, aren't you? Where is this *astounding* invention? And who is the brilliant inventor — yourself?" He laughed again.

"As a matter of fact" — Jonathan pulled himself up to look as dignified as a twelve-year-old in too-short pants could look — "the invention is in my pocket. But I can't show it to anyone except Mr. Lincoln. And the inventor is Mr.

Frank Kenny. I work for him. He would have liked to show his invention to the president himself, except he broke his leg and can't time-travel." *Whoops!* "Can't *travel*."

The usher raised a skeptical eyebrow, but he stepped back. Jonathan slipped through the barely open door without hesitating, and the usher shut and locked it. "Hmph! Well, the president may be in the mood for a hearty laugh," said the usher. "What did you say your name was? Wait here." He disappeared into another room.

Jonathan wandered around the waiting room, thinking guiltily of the mother trying to get a pardon for her son, and the stoic Native Americans, and Corporal Brown with his large family and no pay. Never mind, he told himself. If you don't get to see Lincoln, by tomorrow there won't be any Lincoln for *anyone* to see.

The usher reappeared, chuckling. "President Lincoln will see you now." He held open the next door. "Master Jonathan Schultz," he announced.

Jonathan stopped just inside the door, gaping up at the man holding out his hand. The president's homely face with its unruly dark hair and fringe of beard was as familiar as a five-dollar bill. And yet, it was different from any picture of Abraham Lincoln that Jonathan had ever seen.

Lincoln shook Jonathan's hand gently. Jonathan himself had fairly big hands, with long fingers, but the president's hands were huge, like those of a basketball player. "Take a chair" (he pronounced it "cheer"), said Lincoln. "What have you got to show me, Jonathan?" With an awkward kind of folding-up motion, Lincoln sat down on a sofa. The way he moved reminded Jonathan of his own gawkiness, except that Jonathan hoped *he* was just going through a phase.

Perching on the edge of a chair opposite the sofa, Jonathan tried to collect his thoughts. He'd never in his life met anyone famous. Now here he was, a few feet from *Abraham Lincoln*. His brain flickered, like a failing computer screen.

President Lincoln's face was sallow and tired, but his eyes gleamed with interest. "I hear you've brought an invention — what was the word? — an *astounding* invention."

Jonathan mentally shook himself. Get a grip, Schultz! "That's right, sir." He put a hand on his pocket, and the flat shape of the TASC remote control seemed to calm him. "I'll show it to you in a minute." He cleared his throat and began to explain.

Crossing one long leg over the other knee, Lincoln listened patiently as Jonathan described what the TASC was and how it worked. Jonathan wasn't sure how much technology Lincoln knew, so he just talked as if he were talking to Mr. Kenny. Once Lincoln interrupted with a question about the special properties of rose quartz crystals, and another time with a question about the curvature of the space-time matrix. Finally he commented, "Sounds to me like you travel through time the way a message travels through a telegraph wire."

"Exactly!" exclaimed Jonathan. This dude is really smart, he thought in amazement. He isn't just honest and good, those things they always tell you about Lincoln. "Of course there isn't any wire," he added. "That's the function performed by the crystal."

"Of course." The president grinned suddenly, showing surprisingly white, even teeth. "Son, I have to hand it to you. I consider myself a real fine storyteller. But you beat me all to thunder." He guffawed, slapping his knee. "Traveling through time! That's the best tall tale I've ever heard."

Jonathan's spirits sank as he watched Lincoln rock back and forth, hugging his knee and whooping with laughter. "Please, Mr. President. You have to believe me! The reason I came here from the future is to tell you not to go to Ford's Theater tonight. Somebody's going to try to *kill* you."

Jonathan started to describe John Wilkes Booth's plan, but Lincoln, suddenly serious, held up a hand. "Wait, Jonathan. Let me show you something."

Unfolding himself from the sofa, the president ambled over to a desk against the wall. From one of the drawers he took a large envelope, bulging with papers. "These are threats against my life." He pulled a note from the envelope, put on wire-rimmed glasses, and read out loud, " 'To APE-KING Lincoln: You had better say yer prayers be cause you do not have much longer in this world.' "

Lincoln lowered his head to look at Jonathan over his glasses. "That's a fair sample — there are dozens like it. Why, there are more people who want to kill me than who want me to give them a job in the government!"

The president seemed to mean that as a joke, but Jonathan didn't laugh. "But sir, isn't that all the more — "

"Son, I take your concern for me kindly, very kindly. But I don't need a visitor from the future to tell me that some people wish me dead. That's been the way of it, ever since I came to Washington. Once a fellow took a potshot at me while I was out riding — ruined a perfectly good top hat!" Lincoln's finger traced the path of a bullet an inch above his head.

"But I can tell you exactly what's going to happen and who's going to do it," urged Jonathan. "It's a man named — "

"If it is to be, it will be," said Lincoln quietly. "Jonathan, did you ever visit Niagara Falls?"

"No." Jonathan let out an impatient sigh. What was the president getting at? "I've seen pictures."

"Well, then, you have some idea of the force of the torrent rushing over those cliffs. The force of fate is like that." President Lincoln spoke calmly, his eyes looking over Jonathan's head as if he were seeing some far horizon. "You can throw a pebble into Niagara Falls, but it won't stop the water from falling. Won't change anything, not so you'd notice it."

Jonathan swallowed hard. Maybe Lincoln would listen to him if he could *prove* that the Time and Space Connector really worked. It was risky. He shouldn't use the TASC by himself, especially without consulting Matt and Emily. But if a demonstration of time travel was the only thing that would convince Lincoln, it would be worth it. "Sir, let me *show* you how I travel in time."

"I would enjoy that mightily," said Lincoln. He sat back down on the sofa and folded his arms, as if he were waiting for a performance to begin.

"Great, but I can't leave from here." Jonathan jumped up. "We have to go to the street in front of Ford's Theater, because that's where — "

Lincoln burst out laughing. "Very ingenious!" Rising again, he put a friendly hand on Jonathan's shoulder and guided him toward the door.

"I surely would like to see you shoot through an invisible telegraph wire, if Mrs. Lincoln didn't expect me for lunch." He opened the door for Jonathan.

Jonathan couldn't believe it. He'd failed. He was about to step out the door, stunned, when he remembered his promise. "Wait! One more thing." He told the president about Corporal Joshua Brown not getting his pay.

Going back to his desk, Lincoln made a note. "I'll have that taken care of." He looked up over his glasses again, and Jonathan was sure that the president's opinion of him had gone up a notch. "I'll tell you what: come around again Monday afternoon at three. My son Tad and I are going to the Smithsonian to watch an experiment."

"I — I'd like to, very much," stammered Jonathan.

Lincoln nodded, and a smile creased his tired face. "Good-bye, son."

6.
"The Secretary Is Generally Right"

Retracing his way into the hall and down the stairs and through the first floor of the White House, Jonathan kept hearing the president's last word to him. *Son.*

Jonathan wished, so hard that it hurt, that he could come back Monday afternoon and spend some more time with homely, gangly, smart, kindly President Lincoln. He'd never felt so much at home with any adult, except for Mr. Kenny. Maybe there was some way . . .

At the front door, the doorman winked at him. "How was your meeting with the president, young fellow — satisfactory?"

Jonathan knew that the doorman was kidding him, but the question shook him out of his daze. "No," he said slowly. "Not really." What had gone wrong? Jonathan had been incredibly lucky — out of all those people waiting, he'd gotten in to see Lincoln. He'd shaken the president's hand. He'd warned Lincoln about the plot to kill him tonight. But all that was only a pebble in Niagara Falls, as Lincoln put it. Nothing had changed!

He'd better get on to the next leg of his mission. "Now I have to find the War Department. Isn't that right around here somewhere?"

The doorman chuckled. "I suppose you're going to speak with the secretary of war next? That's the spirit. You'll find Mr. Stanton next door, in that red brick building." He stepped out on the porch to point across the wide stretch of lawn. "Now that the war's won, you might even find the secretary in a good humor."

The warm breeze lifted the hair on Jonathan's forehead as he walked back down the White House drive to the gates. He wished he'd had more time to discuss this part of his mission with Matt. But Jonathan was pretty sure his time-travel story would be even more useless with Secretary of War Stanton than with President Lincoln. Better to say he'd overheard some guys in a bar, talking about this plot to kill the president.

The War Department building had sentries posted all around, and one of them challenged Jonathan as he neared the front steps. When he mentioned a plot to kill the president, though, a soldier hustled him in the front door and down the hall to an office.

The sentry let go of Jonathan's collar to salute

the officer at the desk. "This here young puppy says he knows of a conspiracy, sir. Overheard it in a barroom, sir."

The officer narrowed his eyes at Jonathan. "Boys who hang around barrooms come to no good end — don't you know that?" He pointed to a bench against the wall. "Sit down."

"I wasn't hanging around," protested Jonathan. "I was — I was delivering a message."

But the officer ignored him. Dismissing the sentry with a nod, he picked up a stack of papers and walked across the hall. Jonathan caught some of what he said. "Mr. Secretary, sir. . . . Orders for the execution of twelve deserters . . . pardons from the president . . . Oh, and I have in my office a boy who . . . I thought you might wish to . . ."

Jonathan leaned back on the bench, wondering whether the brother and son of the women he'd seen in the White House was on that list of deserters from the army. If Jonathan hadn't pushed his way in, would those women have gotten to see the president and talk him into pardoning their Ben? It didn't seem likely, but he felt guilty again anyway.

A while later, the officer returned and beckoned Jonathan from the doorway. "Come along. But you'd better not be wasting the secretary's time. He's a very important man, and you're nothing but a young rascal, do you understand?"

Nice way to talk to a guy bringing the most important information of the century, thought Jonathan, but he nodded as he stood up. Before they could cross the hall, though, a tall, gangly figure in a rumpled suit, followed by a burly young man, stepped into the War Department. The officer backed up and saluted smartly, and President Lincoln nodded.

Then Lincoln disappeared into Stanton's office. They heard his twangy drawl. "Mr. Secretary, may I take a minute of your time? I heard a little story about . . ."

The door closed, and the voices across the hall became a murmur. With a shrug, the officer motioned Jonathan back to the bench. "If the president wants to tell the secretary a little story, we may as well settle down to wait." To the burly man who had come with Lincoln he called, "Sit down in here if you like, Mr. Crook."

"Thank you, lieutenant." Mr. Crook, a young man with a serious, honest face, stepped into the office and took a seat at the end of the bench. "Just so I keep a clear view of the hall," he explained.

Shuffling some papers on his table, the lieutenant looked at him curiously. "It must not be easy, guarding a man who doesn't take any interest in his own safety."

Crook shook his head gloomily. "Not easy, no — impossible, you might say. It was a miracle

71

that no attempt on his life was made at Richmond last week."

The lieutenant nodded. "The secretary of war was perfectly furious about that. The very idea of President Lincoln visiting Richmond, the capital of the South — just defeated — every white man, woman, and child in the city wishing the president dead!" He lowered his voice. "Do you know what the secretary said about Mr. Lincoln? He said, 'That fool!' "

Crook looked disapproving, but he laughed in spite of himself. "Never mind keeping it low; it's already gotten back to the president. Do you know what *he* said?" Trying to imitate Lincoln's high-pitched twang, Crook went on, " 'If Mr. Stanton said the president is a fool, it must be so, for the secretary is generally right.' "

The lieutenant and Crook chuckled. Then Crook's face turned serious again, and his gaze flicked aside to scan the hall. In a low tone he said, "I tell you, lieutenant, I'd lay down my life for him, just like that." He snapped his fingers.

Jonathan believed him. Mr. Crook reminded him of a dog, one of those big chesty dogs that would die defending its master.

The lieutenant's smile vanished, too. "It may come to that, yet," he said gravely. "We have intelligence about a dozen plots to overthrow the government, and here's one more." He pointed to Jonathan.

Crook turned to stare at the boy sitting at the other end of the bench. "Bless my soul! A whippersnapper like this, plotting against the president?"

"Not me," protested Jonathan. "I came here to *tell* Mr. Stanton about a plot."

"You'd better tell the truth, then." Crook gave Jonathan a hard stare. "The secretary has a very short temper."

"Extremely short," agreed the lieutenant. "He'd thrash you as soon as look at you."

Jonathan was pretty sure they were trying to scare him. Still, he wasn't looking forward much to his interview with Secretary of War Stanton.

The bodyguard pulled a watch almost as big as a computer mouse from his coat pocket. As he glanced at it, Jonathan managed to read the time — it was after three o'clock. Oh, no! What about checking in with Matt and Emily? He really ought to tell them that he didn't get anywhere with Lincoln. Well, a chance to talk to Stanton was much more important. Maybe it wouldn't take that long.

Dropping his watch back in his pocket, Crook started to say something. But he paused at the sound of the door across the hall opening. The lieutenant cocked his head, too, and all three of them listened.

"Now, you're sure you won't join us at the theater tonight, Mr. Secretary?" asked Lincoln.

"Mr. President, I *never* attend the theater."
Stanton's voice was full of disapproval.

"And furthermore" — the lieutenant leaned
over his table to whisper to Crook — "Mrs. Stanton wouldn't attend *any* place if she knew Mrs.
Lincoln was going to be there. Not after the way
she was insulted . . ."

"Well, then," Lincoln was saying, "let Tom
Eckert off for the evening to come with me. You
can't keep him shackled to the telegraph key
day and night."

"I cannot spare Eckert just now," Stanton said
stiffly. "Good day, Mr. President."

"It is a good day," said Lincoln good-
humoredly. "In case you change your mind, I'll
leave this ticket for Tom Eckert."

Jumping up from the bench, Crook trotted
down the hall after the gangly man in the top
hat. Then Stanton called from his office, "Well,
bring the boy *in*, lieutenant," as if they'd been
keeping the secretary of war waiting instead of
the other way around.

The lieutenant led Jonathan across the hall.
"This is the boy, sir."

The first thing Jonathan noticed about the
man standing behind a high desk was his beard.
Unlike Lincoln's, Stanton's beard was long and
curly, dark but with a gray streak flowing down
from his lower lip. His upper lip was clean-
shaven. The hair receding from his forehead was

curly, too. The secretary wore wire-rimmed glasses, through which he fixed a piercing gaze on Jonathan.

Stanton motioned the lieutenant to a table. "Take down the interview." He turned back to Jonathan. "Name? Address?"

As Jonathan answered the questions the secretary of war rapped out, the lieutenant dipped his pen in an inkwell and wrote rapidly. Jonathan told his story about overhearing four men in a saloon whispering plans to shoot the president at Ford's Theater this evening.

Stanton leaned forward on his high desk, his eyes boring into Jonathan as if to discover, just by staring at him, whether he was telling the truth. "Did you know these men?"

"I recognized one of them," Jonathan answered. His heart beat faster — it seemed he'd almost accomplished his mission. Once the secretary of war knew about the plot, Jonathan and Matt and Emily could relax. You could see that Stanton was the kind of guy who'd have Booth thrown into prison before you could say "Johnny Reb."

"Spit it out, boy." Stanton drummed his fingers on the desktop. "Who was it?"

"John Wilkes Booth."

The secretary of war turned his fierce stare on his assistant. The lieutenant, his face flushing, put down his pen. "I'm afraid I've wasted your time, sir. The boy must have been put up to this by another actor, someone with a grudge against Booth."

Why were they so sure? Jonathan didn't get it. "It *was* Booth," he protested. "I'd know him anywhere."

Stanton gave a short, humorless laugh. "Whoever sent you might have found an easier way to harm Mr. Booth. Consider: Is it at all likely that the most popular actor in the nation, a wealthy man with a career and a fortune to lose, would consider such a desperate act?" Scowling at Jonathan, he drummed his fingers again. "Still," he went on to the lieutenant, "we can't afford to ignore even the wildest stories. Put a man on Booth."

"I believe Mr. Booth is staying at the National Hotel," said the lieutenant, "and Porter is already watching another suspect there."

"Yes, yes," said Stanton impatiently. "Have Porter keep an eye on Booth, too." With a wave of dismissal, he picked up a paper on his desk. Then a thought seemed to strike him, and he held out a small piece of cardboard to Jonathan. "I suppose you expected a reward for your trouble, boy. Here it is. The theater is the right place for rapscallions."

The lieutenant hustled Jonathan out of Stanton's office. "Don't you ever show your face around the War Department again. What a cock-and-bull story!" He handed Jonathan over to the sentry in the hall, who pushed him out onto the porch.

Stalking away from the War Department, Jonathan raged to himself. Nice security system, Mr. Secretary of War! Oh, way to go, protecting the president! Mr. Lincoln thinks you're "generally right" — well, you're wrong *this* time.

By the time Jonathan reached the iron fence of the White House grounds, he'd calmed down a bit. It didn't really matter whether Stanton believed Jonathan or not, if his mission was accomplished. But was it, or wasn't it? They weren't going to do what he'd hoped — arrest Booth. On the other hand, one of their men was going to watch Booth — sort of.

Now, what? wondered Jonathan. It must be about four o'clock. But he should go to the Washington Monument anyway, in case Matt and Emily were still waiting for him.

Gazing all around the low horizon through the misty air, Jonathan saw treetops and church spires and a stubby tower and the distant dome of the Capitol. But nowhere did he see the tall white shaft of the Washington Monument. How could Matt be so wrong, saying you could spot the monument from anywhere in the city? He climbed a tree to get a better view, but still no monument.

Jonathan felt a twinge of worry. He really should check in with Matt and Emily. Stopping a soldier, he asked directions. The man didn't know; he'd just come to town with General Grant's troops. But a woman passing by overheard them and directed Jonathan down Seventeenth Street. "On the other side of the canal," she explained.

She sounded like she knew what she was talking about, but when Jonathan got to the bottom of Seventeenth Street, he didn't even bother crossing the smelly canal. Nothing but mud flats and cattle pens on the other side. Anyway, it was probably too late to meet Matt and Emily. He'd look for them at Ford's Theater.

Wandering back down Pennsylvania Avenue, Jonathan caught a whiff of meat roasting somewhere. Maybe it was the dinner cooking in the White House kitchen. He thought of a noble sacrifice he'd made for his mission, completely unappreciated by everyone, including the secretary of war and his staff: Jonathan had skipped lunch.

There was a sudden cool gust of wind, and raindrops spattered the boards of the sidewalk. The other people out walking stopped to put up umbrellas. Jonathan hunched his shoulders and hurried down the street, looking for shelter. He paused under the marble porch of the Treasury building, getting hungrier by the minute.

In a short while the rain stopped, but the sun stayed behind the clouds. Jonathan started down the street again, thinking of the story he'd made up for the lieutenant about delivering a message. Maybe he could actually deliver a message to earn some 1865 money — enough money to buy something to eat.

Jonathan peered down a side street. In the damp gray afternoon, the doorway of a saloon glowed yellow under an arched sign: *Harvey's*. Harvey's seemed to be more than a place to drink — a wonderful seafood smell poured out the door along with the yellow light. Trying not to drool, Jonathan hurried toward the saloon.

Many men must have been drawn in the same way Jonathan was, because the bar was very crowded. And what a bar — it seemed to stretch on forever down the long room, almost disappearing into the cigar smoke. Jonathan coughed, but he wasn't going to let a little smoke bother him. His eyes followed the plates of steamed oysters, still on the shell, which waiters were setting down before the men at the bar. Plates of oysters, baskets of thick crackers.

Squirming through the crowd to the bar, Jonathan watched a stout man in front of him pour sauce from a bottle onto his oysters, pick them up one at a time, and slide them into his mouth. He took a swig from his mug of beer. "Ah!"

Next to the fat man, a man with muttonchop

whiskers raised his glass and looked around. "A toast, boys! Here's to General Grant, for beating the Rebs all to thunder!"

Hands holding glasses went up all around him. "To General Grant!"

The fat man beside Jonathan hoisted his glass again. "And here's to Uncle Billy Sherman!"

"To General Sherman!"

The glasses were emptying fast, and the bartenders scurried to refill them. Jonathan tapped the fat man on the shoulder. "Excuse me, sir. Do you have any message to deliver? All I'd ask for it is some crackers."

The man turned his jowly face toward Jonathan. "Deliver messages, eh?" He nudged the man next to him. "What do you say, shall we send a message to Jefferson Davis? 'To Mr. Davis, former president of the former Confederacy: I regret to inform you that the Union has won the war.' Three cheers for Old Abe!"

Up and down the bar, the men raised their glasses again. "To President Lincoln — hip, hip, hurrah!"

Jonathan joined in the cheers, but he felt himself becoming skinnier and skinnier. He wondered if he could sneak a cracker from the basket when no one was looking.

But when the fat man set down his mug, he beamed at Jonathan. "Here, boy, belly up to the bar." He spoke to the waiter. "Give this boy a plate of oysters and a mug of your best sarsa-parilla. And I'll have another plate, myself."

A moment later Jonathan was gulping down oysters (they weren't bad when you doused them with the sauce) and crackers. He paused to raise his mug of soda with the rest of them. "To General Grant! To General Sherman! To Old Abe and his next four years in the White House!"

7.
Bad Dreams

Leaving Jonathan in front of the White House, Matt tried to ignore a pang of envy. He wished, much more than he'd admitted to Jonathan, that *he* could have been the one to talk to President Lincoln. Of course, Jonathan had to take that mission; no question. Matt could just imagine himself trying to explain time travel to President Lincoln: "Well, you see, sir, we stand in front of the projector, and Jonathan does something with the thingy, and . . . I don't have a clue how it happens."

But to be right here in Washington in 1865, and miss the chance to meet *Abraham Lincoln*!

Forget it, Matt told himself. The important thing was saving Lincoln, so each of the kids had to do what they could do best. Matt strode briskly across the lawn and into the gardens. He was heading for the back of the White House to look for some kind of servants' entrance.

Maybe he could pretend he was related to one of the employees.

As Matt rounded a bank of lilac bushes in full bloom, he tried to ignore his growling stomach. Why hadn't they remembered to bring snacks? Somehow, wearing these ragged clothes made Matt feel hungrier than usual, as if he were really poor and didn't get enough to eat. He tried to steer his mind away from food and toward a good explanation for why he wanted to talk to the Lincoln family. Maybe he'd say he was psychic, that he'd had a premonition about danger to the president.

"Ha!" A small person in uniform, waving a sword, leaped out from behind the lilacs. "Ha, I say!"

Startled, Matt stumbled backward. Then he stared, not knowing whether to laugh or not. This person playing sentry was a boy — about ten years old, he thought, or even younger. But was that a real sword?

Under the bill of the Union Army cap, there was a gleeful light in the boy's round eyes. "Give your name, sir," he commanded. At least, Matt *thought* that's what he said. The boy's words were difficult to understand, as if he had the world's worst cold *and* was eating a peanut-butter sandwich.

"I'm Matt Cowen. Hey, careful with that

sword!" The gleaming blade a few inches from Matt's neck was not plastic, or even painted wood. It was genuine steel.

With a sudden grin, the boy lowered his sword. "Don't be scared. I'm Tad Lincoln. But this is a real officer's uniform. Mr. Stanton gave it to me. He's secretary of war, you know." Tad's eyes focused on Matt's ragged clothes, and his smile faded into concern. "Are you hungry?"

Matt hesitated. But why not tell the truth? "*Yes.*"

A smile lit up Tad's mischievous face again. "Come on, I'll tell them to give you some lunch."

As Tad led Matthew around toward the back of the White House, he chattered on. "My brother Robert is a *real* officer in the army, with General Grant. Robert saw General Lee surrender, and that meant the Union had won the war. And Robert came home this morning and showed Papa a picture of General Lee, and Papa said, 'It is a good face. I am glad that the war is over.' "

A small door at the back of the building led through a pantry into a warm, steamy kitchen. A woman with a kerchief on her head was stirring a pot on the big cast-iron stove. Another woman worked at a long table, cutting biscuits out of a sheet of floured dough. As Matt followed Tad into the room, the woman at the stove turned and wiped sweat from her forehead with her apron.

From the way she frowned at them, Matt thought the cook was going to chase them out of the kitchen. But Tad announced in his cheerful stuffed-up voice, "This is a poor hungry boy! Give him an *enormous* plate of lunch, please."

"Here, Master Tad," the woman said gruffly, "we can't allus be feedin' all the ragamuffins you drag in off the street." But she filled a plate and motioned Matt to a stool in the corner. "Ain't you s'pose to be studyin' your lessons?" she asked Tad. "You twelve years old, and hardly readin' and writin' yet! Where's your tutor at?"

Biting into a chunk of corn bread dripping with butter, Matt stared at Tad. This kid was twelve, Matt and Jonathan's age? He hardly looked as old as Emily. Or maybe it was more that he *acted* like a much younger kid.

Tad giggled at the cook and rubbed the row of brass buttons on the front of his uniform. "I fooled my tutor. He thinks I'm in the library. He's not a bad fellow, though," he went on to Matt. "He's taking me to the theater tonight. Do you like the theater? I have my own theater, right in the White House. My papa loves the theater. He and Mama are going to Ford's to see *Our American Cousin* tonight, but I'm going to see *Aladdin*."

"*Aladdin*'s at the National Theater, right?" asked Matt through a mouthful of chicken stew. "I saw the poster for that play." The mention of the theater reminded him of his mission, and he put down his fork. "Hey, Tad, do you know that dreams can foretell the future?"

To Matt's surprise, Tad's face turned pale. "Don't say that! Papa had a very bad dream, just last week." Tad's lower lip trembled, and he stared past Matt as he went on. "Papa dreamed he woke up at night and walked through the house. And the lights were all lit, and he heard people sobbing. And when he came to the East Room, there was someone dead, laid out for a funeral."

"Don' talk like that, Master Tad," urged the cook. A worried frown creased her forehead. "Don' give an evil dream the power that way, by talkin' 'bout it."

Tad took a breath and went on as if she hadn't spoken. "And Papa asked, 'Who is dead in the White House?' And they said — " A shudder ran through Tad's body. "They said, 'The president!' "

Matt shuddered, too, but he felt this was his chance. "*I* had a bad dream last night," he said. "That's why I came to the White House, to warn all of you. I dreamed that someone is going to try to shoot your father at Ford's — "

"Don't say that!" shouted Tad. He put his hands over his ears.

The cook scowled at Matt. "No good ain't gon'

come from draggin' trash into my kitchen and lettin' 'em — "

"But listen, Tad," Matt pleaded. "What if you asked your father to take you to *Aladdin* tonight, instead of — " Matt broke off. A woman swept into the kitchen, giving instructions to the cook before she was through the doorway.

This woman was short and plump, but she carried herself like — like a queen, thought Matt. Her purple dress, with enough material in the skirt for a bedspread, was elegantly cut, and there was a gold and ivory pin in the black lace at the high-necked throat. "A clear soup tonight, I think," she was saying to the cook. "And as for the fish — " She caught sight of Tad. "Why, Taddie. How could you? You are supposed to be at your lessons with your tutor."

Tad flashed a mischievous grin at her. "I gave him the slip again, Mama."

So this was Mary Lincoln, thought Matt. Her shiny hair was smoothed back into a bun from a straight center part, and she had a thin, determined-looking mouth. But her eyes as she gazed at Tad were soft and warm.

"Mrs. Lincoln, ma'am," the cook spoke up. "I surely don' like to complain, ma'am, but Master Tad has been draggin' urchins in off the streets again."

Mrs. Lincoln turned to Matt, running her eyes

over his tattered clothes. He jumped up, holding his plate, and made a little bow. "Thank you very much for the lunch, ma'am."

"Mama," said Tad, "Matt was *so* hungry. You know that Papa and Mr. Seward both told me I was right to feed poor people."

Mrs. Lincoln smiled fondly at her son. "So tenderhearted — just like your papa." She nodded graciously at Matt. "And this boy has nice manners, even if he is poor."

"I know, Mama," said Tad eagerly. "Do you know who he reminds me of? He reminds me of our Wil — "

Matt glanced from Mrs. Lincoln to Tad and back again. He was amazed that *anything* could make Tad stop talking in the middle of a sentence. But even before Tad stopped, Matt had seen Mrs. Lincoln flinch, as if she knew what her son was going to say.

There had been another Lincoln boy, Matt remembered. Willie, the one who'd died in the White House, of typhoid fever. Probably from drinking the unsanitary water they used to have in Washington.

Mary Lincoln pressed her lips together and blinked, as if she was forcing back tears. She patted Matt's shoulder. "Cook will give you a packet of corn bread to take with you. And Taddie, run and fetch Robert's old school jacket for this boy. You know the chest where I keep the old clothes, where you rummage for costumes."

While Tad was gone, Matt sat back on his stool and finished his lunch. Mrs. Lincoln conferred with the cook about what was to be had in the market, and about something special for dessert tonight, to tempt Mr. Lincoln's appetite. Then Tad returned with a jacket, which Matt put on with many thanks. He felt like a fraud, thinking of his closet full of clothes and his kitchen full of food back home. Still, he *had* been hungry, and it *did* look like rain.

"Mrs. Lincoln," Matt spoke up as she turned to leave the room, "I came to tell you something important." As he paused, Mary Lincoln turned back with a swirl of her full skirts. The smile on her face faded, as if she was afraid of what he might say.

Matt hesitated, feeling Mary Lincoln's dread. It seemed cruel to tell this woman whose son had died that her husband was about to die, too. He almost felt that maybe if he didn't say anything, it wouldn't happen. But he took a deep breath. This was what he'd come for. "Please don't let President Lincoln go to Ford's Theater tonight."

"Mama!" Tad clutched his mother's hand. "Matt dreamed they shot Papa dead!"

Mrs. Lincoln's plump face quivered as if it were going to fall apart. "No!" she exclaimed. "Hush! No!"

"I did *tell* Master Tad, ma'am," the cook put in, "ain't no good gon' come — "

"I didn't make it up," Matt insisted. But he felt so bad, he almost wished he hadn't said anything.

Pressing Tad to her, Mrs. Lincoln stared reproachfully at Matt. "We have shown you charity, and in return, you torment us with our sorrows and fears. The theater is Mr. Lincoln's only recreation. The war has made him old and sick. Were you sent by one of his enemies who wants him to have no rest?"

"It — it's not like that," stammered Matt. "I just don't want President — "

"Stop!" Mrs. Lincoln shut her eyes and put her hands to both sides of her sleekly combed hair, as if she were getting a headache. "I will not hear any more." Whirling so that her hoopskirt swung, she pulled Tad out of the kitchen. The sword hanging from the boy's belt clattered against the legs of chairs on his way out.

The cook scowled at Matt and raised a rolling pin. Taking the hint, he scurried out through the pantry. He hadn't had a chance to talk to Robert Lincoln, Tad's older brother, but it didn't look like he was going to. This mission had failed.

Stepping outside, Matt was glad he'd taken the jacket. The air felt chillier, after the warm kitchen, and the clouds looked lower and darker.

Matt stood in the garden for a moment, remembering the haunted look in Mary Lincoln's eyes. It was as if she already knew, but refused to accept, what was going to happen.

But it *wouldn't*! Matt and Emily and Jonathan would stop it, somehow.

Now Matt was anxious to check in with Emily and Jonathan, to see if they'd had any luck with their missions. Matt had noticed the time on the kitchen clock: almost three. The Washington Monument, where the kids were supposed to meet at three o'clock, was down by the river.

Matt wasn't sure how long it would take to walk there — he'd better hurry. He certainly didn't want to miss meeting the others. He remembered all too well how they'd gotten separated last trip, visiting the American Revolution in 1775. He'd spent half the time worried sick about whether Emily or Jonathan was lying dead somewhere.

To get his bearings, Matt walked over to the back entrance of the White House, just as palace-like as the front. He climbed the broad steps and stood among the pillars, gazing out over the treetops. There was a canal, a stretch of flat land, and beyond that, the Potomac River.

Matt frowned. He knew the monument was between the White House and the river. And he knew it was over 500 feet tall. He'd personally climbed to the top, the time his family had visited Washington. But the only structure of any height in that direction was a stumpy tower. Oh, well. He could head toward the river and ask somebody.

Returning to the sidewalk in front of the White House, Matt hurried on, past the cannon on the lawn of the War Department building. He thought of stopping to check on Jonathan. No — Jonathan and Secretary of War Stanton would probably get along better without him. Besides, Jonathan might already be waiting for Matt at the monument.

After Matt turned the corner onto Seventeenth Street, it was only a few minutes' walk to the foot of that broad, tree-lined avenue. Seventeenth Street ended on the bank of the canal.

Matt smelled the canal before he saw the water. It smelled the way the Cowens' yard had smelled last fall, when there was a problem with the septic tank — only much worse. Like a sewer.

Trying to breathe through his mouth, Matt peered over the bank at the murky, sluggish stream. He swallowed, feeling a little sick. No wonder Willie Lincoln had died of typhoid, if this was what sanitary conditions were like here. Matt hoped Emily and Jonathan had remembered his warning not to drink the water.

Anyway, where *was* the Washington Monument? Matt knew for a fact that they'd laid the

cornerstone in 1848 — it had to be here somewhere. But on this side of the canal, below the
White House, there was only a parklike area,
with nothing taller than the trees. On the other
side of the canal, a flat, grassy plain merged into
marsh and then the river. Nothing tall out there,
unless you counted the stumpy tower he'd noticed before.

He'd just have to ask. Crossing a bridge over
the canal, Matt walked past cattle pens to the
sheds near the foot of the tower. There was
a powerful aroma of barnyard over here, but
after the sewer-canal stench, it smelled fine to
Matt.

A man in a light blue uniform leaned on a
fence, talking with the cattle herder. One of his
trouser legs, with a dark stripe down the side,
flapped around a wooden peg.

"Excuse me, sir," said Matt to the soldier. "I'm
looking for the Washington Monument. Could
you tell me where it is?"

Exchanging glances, the soldier and the cattleman burst out laughing. "I kin tell you where
part of it is," said the soldier.

In sudden understanding, Matt stared over
the roofs of the long sheds, up at the stone tower.
Now he noticed the scaffolding on top. This was
not the soaring white spire he'd expected, but it
was the Washington Monument of Civil War
days.

8.
Mr. Booth's Plan

"**S**o they haven't finished it yet," said Matt, still staring up at the stump of the Washington Monument. It bothered him just to look at it.

"No, I reckon they spent all the money on bullets and cannonballs." The soldier waved a hand at the monument base. "Them marble blocks don't come three for a penny."

"Besides" — the cattleman paused to squirt a stream of tobacco juice onto the ground — "what's the use of puttin' up a monument to the Father of our Country, if you don't know if there's going to *be* a consarned country?"

"That's jest it," agreed the soldier. "Ole Abe pulled us through, but the Union came mighty close to busting all to pieces — mighty close."

"You mean, like at Gettysburg?" asked Matt.

"Gettysburg was a close one." The soldier nodded grimly. "I wasn't at Gettysburg myself, but I heared about it."

"If you *had* been at Gettysburg," remarked the cattleman, "likely you'd *still* be there — underground."

That seemed like a depressing joke to Matt, but the men both laughed. "Yes, sir," the soldier went on. "Over twenty thousand Union dead, at Gettysburg. Seein' as I lost a leg at Fort Stevens" — he lifted his wooden peg — "I sure as shootin' would have lost my life at Gettysburg."

"Fort Stevens?" asked Matt. "Where's that?" He knew a lot about the Civil War, but he hadn't heard of that battle.

"Too durn close," said the cattleman. "Last July, it was, right up there in them hills." He turned away from the river to point up beyond the city.

Matt stared up at the hills, covered with farm fields and patches of woods. The Confederate Army had come *that* close to capturing Washington. He could imagine the deep mutter of cannon, the columns of smoke from burning farmhouses — only a few miles from the capital of the United States.

The soldier, happy to have an audience, launched into one war story after the other. Matt climbed onto the fence and settled down to listen. There was a funny story about how the soldier's company had conducted a funeral service for the rotten meat they were served. There was a horrendous story about the slaughter at the

Battle of Chancellorsville. There was a sad story about the soldier spotting his cousin in a gray Confederate uniform across the battle lines.

Finally, though, Matt's eyes strayed past the soldier to the bridges across the canal. Jonathan and Emily were not going to show. What had happened to them? "Excuse me, sir," he asked the soldier, "do you know what time it is?"

"Time to get in out of the rain," said the cattleman, as a gust of cold, damp wind hit them. "The weather's turned again."

The soldier pulled a round watch on a chain from his coat pocket. "Jest about a quarter till five."

Thanking him, Matt hurried back toward the canal. Of course there were several possible reasons why Emily and Jonathan hadn't shown up. Maybe, when they couldn't see the Washington Monument, they'd figured Matt was mistaken about it being there in 1865. Maybe they were caught up in their missions and didn't want to break away.

But there were some other "maybes" that worried Matt. For one thing, he remembered reading that Secretary of War Stanton had a terrible temper. Stanton was in the habit of throwing people into prison on the slightest suspicion. What if Stanton had become suspicious of Jonathan?

An even worse "maybe," about Emily, froze

Matt halfway across the canal bridge. The last time he saw his sister, Matt had been standing across the street from Ford's Theater. A well-dressed young man with a mustache and soulful dark eyes had been helping her up. At the time, Matt had thought there was something familiar about the guy. Now he was afraid he knew who it was: the assassin John Wilkes Booth.

What if Booth had somehow found out that Emily knew of his plot and was trying to stop him? When Emily got mad, she sometimes blurted things out. The thought gave Matt a choked, queasy feeling.

Now Matt was in a hurry to get to Ford's Theater and check up on Emily. Instead of going back up Seventeenth Street, he figured it would be quicker to follow the canal to Fifteenth Street and walk up to Pennsylvania Avenue. From there, he'd retrace his and Jonathan's steps to the theater. Emily should be there. Jonathan might be there, too, as a matter of fact — Ford's Theater would be the logical meeting place, after the Washington Monument.

Turning up Fifteenth Street, Matt quickly found himself in the middle of a slum. Ramshackle houses were crowded by lean-tos and shanties built from scraps of lumber and canvas. From the doorways ragged black children stared at Matt. It struck him that even with his Huck Finn clothes, his shoes and jacket made him the best-dressed boy in this neighborhood.

Still, in the middle of such poverty, there seemed to be a celebration going on. A bonfire was blazing in the middle of the street. A banjo twanged out a rousing tune, backed up by a washtub drum and a rhythm instrument made out of two sticks. The crowd around the bonfire danced and clapped and sang out verse after verse. Every time they came to the chorus, they pointed to a black soldier standing near the musicians, and the soldier smiled proudly. "Joshua fit the battle of Jericho," they sang, "and the walls come tumbling down!"

Matt stood mesmerized. To these people, victory for the North had a special, personal meaning, far more than whether the United States (a country of which they hadn't even been citizens) survived. It meant the difference between being slaves and being free.

Caught up in the spirit of the celebration, Matt let himself be folded into the edge of the crowd. He clapped and swayed and sang the choruses, song after song. But at last he pulled his eyes away from the bonfire and realized that it was almost dark. What was he thinking of? He had to get to the theater and find Jonathan and Emily.

Turning onto Pennsylvania Avenue, Matt hurried past the hotels and saloons and newspaper offices. The celebration was going on here, too. In the deepening evening candles glowed in upper-story windows, and songs were roared from the saloons. "Glory, glory, hallelujah!" was the chorus of one that sounded familiar to Matt.

Back on Tenth Street where the three kids had landed this morning, Matt was about to cross over to Ford's Theater when a small group of men appeared in the center archway. One of them stood out, like a peacock in a flock of pigeons.

That's him, thought Matt. John Wilkes Booth. The snappy dresser in the black outfit, swinging a riding whip as he led the group down the steps. His companions looked like workmen, maybe stagehands, in rumpled old clothes.

Booth, walking around free! This was bad news. So Emily's plan to get Booth arrested had not worked. Neither had Jonathan's second assignment, to persuade Secretary of War Stanton to seize Booth.

Somebody had to keep an eye on Booth and look for a chance to stop him. Maybe Jonathan's or Matt's efforts would prevent Lincoln from going to Ford's Theater tonight, but that wouldn't end the danger. It wouldn't help much if Matt and Emily and Jonathan succeeded only in putting off Lincoln's assassination until the next day, or the next week.

The man who hated Abraham Lincoln disappeared with his workmen companions into the

Star Saloon, next door to the theater. Matt ran across the street and slipped into the saloon after them. He was afraid he'd get thrown out, but no one paid any attention to him. After a quick round of drinks, Booth paid and left by the back door. Matt followed him into the alley, trying to stay in the shadows.

To Matt's dismay, Booth went straight to a stable in the alley and came out with a horse. Now it's hopeless, thought Matt, watching him mount the horse. I'll never keep up with him.

Still, as Booth trotted down the alley to Ninth Street, Matt trotted after him. Fortunately, the traffic was heavy, and Booth couldn't let his horse run. Even so, Matt was soon panting and feeling a stitch in his side. But he kept Booth in sight around the corner onto Pennsylvania Avenue and down the street in the direction of the Capitol. Just as Matt was wondering how much longer he could stand the pace, the actor pulled his horse up at the National Hotel.

Matt watched Booth leave his horse at another stable, then disappear through the columned porch of the hotel. He tried to sneak in after Booth, but the doorman hustled him straight out again. The man shook a gloved forefinger at Matt. "No young ragamuffins in the National, thank you very much!"

Still catching his breath, Matt tried to protest that he had a message to deliver. But the doorman only laughed. "Then use the telegraph office on the corner!"

Matt supposed the only thing to do was wait. He waited on the sidewalk in front of the National Hotel for a long time. He watched carriages pull up to the curb as well-dressed ladies and gentlemen came and went from the hotel, but none of the gentlemen was John Wilkes Booth.

At one point there was a shower of rain. A man selling meat pies let Matt huddle under his awning.

"Is there a back door to the hotel?" Matt finally asked the friendly pie vendor. He explained about his important "message" for Mr. Booth.

"No fear!" laughed the pie man. "Mr. John Wilkes Booth always has his horse brought around front for him. Fond of the limelight, that one. Not that he ain't generous," he added quickly. "He'll give me two bits for a pie and never ask for change."

The night turned misty, making halos around the gaslights on the lampposts. The longer Matt waited, the more uneasy he felt. Had Booth already left on his murderous mission?

Worried as he was about Booth, Matt found himself sneaking glances at the pies on the vendor's tray. He'd have to remember for the next trip (if there was a next trip), that they should bring something they could trade for food.

Then Matt forgot about pies, because a man in a dark suit and high riding boots was stepping onto the porch.

"What did I tell you?" the pie vendor remarked to Matt.

Matt was intent on watching Booth. The actor posed on the porch for a moment, staring into the night with dark, brooding eyes. Then he settled a slouch hat on his head and pulled on gloves. Vaulting onto his horse, Booth trotted up the avenue in the direction of the White House.

Matt dashed after him, glad now that he'd had a chance to rest. At Ninth Street, Booth turned, trotted a few more blocks, and reined in his horse just before a cross street. Matt couldn't help noticing the large building on the far corner; it looked like a giant birthday cake, each of its dozens of windows glowing with candles.

A mounted policeman rode slowly past, touching his hat. "Evening, Mr. Booth." He nodded toward the building across the street, blazing with light. "They're still celebrating the victory in the Patent Office, eh?"

"I wish it may catch fire and burn to the ground." Booth pronounced the words distinctly. Then he jumped off his horse, handing the reins to a boy waiting at the curb. The spurs on his boots jingled as he strode up the steps of a small hotel.

Matt noted the sign in front of the hotel: *Herndon House*. It wasn't nearly as elegant as the National. He followed the actor up to the porch and cautiously opened the door. He didn't want to get kicked out of this hotel, too.

Matt glimpsed Booth's spurred heels disappearing up the stairs. Did he dare follow? The woman at the desk was watching him.

Hearing footsteps on the porch, Matt stepped aside for a white-haired man carrying a wicker hamper. The man set the hamper on the floor and gestured to Matt, wheezing. "Here, boy. *Whew!* There's a nickel in it for you." He motioned for Matt to follow him up the stairs with the hamper.

What luck! thought Matt, seizing the hamper. A perfect excuse to go upstairs.

Of course Booth was out of sight by the time the elderly man, with Matt behind him, had huffed and puffed his way up to the third floor. Pocketing his nickel, Matt tiptoed over the shabby carpet to the end of the hall. He thought he heard voices from behind that door.

Thank goodness for these old-fashioned keyholes. Matt knelt and put his eye to the hole. Oh, this was excellent — he could see most of the room.

Booth stood with his back to the door, but there was no mistaking his movie-star pose. None of the other three men in the room looked anything like a movie star. The young man facing the door was built like a football linebacker, though, with powerful shoulders and chest. He slouched against the wall, watching Booth like a dangerous beast awaiting his master's orders.

Also watching Booth, from in front of the washstand, was a middle-aged man with a scraggly little beard and red eyes. His hands picked nervously at the bottom of his wrinkled jacket. And there was one more man, younger than Booth, half-sitting on the footboard of the bed. His jaw was slack, and he listened to Booth with his mouth open and a little frown on his face.

Matt's heart pounded. This was it — the conspirators.

" — Seward's house at precisely ten o'clock, Lewis," Booth was saying. "Tell them you have a message from the secretary of state's physician which you must deliver personally. When you are shown into his bedroom, *you know what to do*." Booth bore down on these last words so hard that his voice shook.

Lewis's answer was calm. "Reckon I *will* know what to do, captain." He giggled.

Matt shivered. They were going to kill the secretary of state, too?

"And as you act," Booth went on to Lewis, "know that at the very same moment, *I* am striking, as the instrument of God's punishment to the tyrant." As he spoke, he pulled his hand from his coat pocket and opened it. There on his palm lay a small brass pistol, decorated with filigree. It looked like a toy.

"But what if somethin' bad happens to Lewis?" asked the stupid-looking young man. "What if he don't come out?"

"You just wait outside Seward's with the horses, Davy," Booth said sharply. "Be a man! Lewis needs you to lead him out of Washington, so that the two of you can meet me on the other side of the Navy Yard Bridge."

"Mr. Boot'," put in the older man. He had a slight German accent. "Could we haff a liddle nip of brandy, chust to take off the chill?"

"In a moment we will drink a toast," Booth answered sternly. "But George, you understand your part? You will return to your room in the Kirkwood House. At ten o'clock you will go down to Vice President Johnson's room and . . . We will act as one man to avenge the noble South."

All Matt's muscles were stiff with horror. This was worse than he'd realized. Booth wasn't only plotting to assassinate the president — he planned to bring down the entire government of the United States.

Then Matt shook himself. What was he doing, staying here at the keyhole? It didn't do any good for *him* to listen to them making their blood-thirsty plans. Matt had to run and get the police.

Now, right away. Before it was too late.

Jumping up, Matt caught his heel on a rip in the carpet and stumbled backward. He grabbed the door handle to steady himself — and the handle rattled.

The murmur of voices inside the room broke off. Matt held his breath and began to tiptoe away, willing them to go on. But someone called out sharply, "Who's there?"

The next moment, the door was flung open. The muscular Lewis pounced on Matt, grabbed him by the back of his jacket collar, and yanked him into the room.

Booth looked shaken, but he gave a scornful laugh. "A Union spy — a boy." To Matt he rapped out, "Who sent you?"

"We ain't got time for that," said Lewis, his steely fingers digging into Matt's shoulder. "You'd best let me wring his neck." His tone of voice was as casual as if Matt had been a chicken.

"No," Booth said sharply. "Our noble cause will not be sullied with ignoble deeds. Shut him in the wardrobe."

"I'd sure wring his neck, if it was up to me." Lewis shrugged. Hustling Matt up to a sort of freestanding closet with a lock on the door, he shoved him inside. Matt heard the key turn.

"Now," said Booth in a dramatic voice, "before we depart — a toast, men." There was a sound of a cork popping out of a bottle. "To the South!" declaimed John Wilkes Booth. "Death to her enemies! Glory to her heroes!"

9.
"Stop That Man!"

It was seven-thirty by the time Jonathan walked out of Harvey's Oyster Saloon, feeling guilty about having enjoyed himself so much. He'd stuffed himself with oysters and crackers. He'd showed the men some simple science-class tricks, like the one where you fill a glass with water and put a piece of cardboard on top and turn it over, and the water stays in the glass. They'd liked that one. Jonathan had also learned some new songs: "Captain Jinks of the Horse Marines," "Shoo, Fly, Don't Bother Me," and "Nine Men Slept in a Boardinghouse Bed." He'd learned *all* the verses to "The Battle Hymn of the Republic."

The night had turned cold and misty. Shivering in his thin clothes, Jonathan envied the other people on the streets, wearing real coats. Also, now he was worried. He should have left the saloon earlier and tried to find Matt and Emily at the theater, the next logical meeting place. Unless Matt or Emily had been completely successful, they all needed to discuss what to do next.

Jonathan hoped the other two kids would be able to get into the theater. It wasn't likely that they'd been as lucky as he in getting a ticket. He felt in his jacket pocket for his ticket to *Our American Cousin*. President Lincoln didn't know Jonathan had ended up with the ticket he'd left on Stanton's desk, but Jonathan liked to think Lincoln would have been glad.

Outside Ford's Theater, the crowd was streaming into the arched entryways. Carriages and buggies pulled up to the curb to let out more theatergoers. Looking around this busy stretch of Tenth Street, Jonathan wondered if it was going to be as dangerous to leave 1865 as it had been to land.

Anyway, there was no sign of Matt or Emily on either side of the street. Joining the flow of the crowd, Jonathan gave his ticket to the ticket taker and went down the center aisle, past the pillars supporting the balcony. The theater was filling up fast, but Jonathan found a single seat in the middle of a row on the left.

It was a good thing Jonathan was skinny, because he had to wedge himself in between a hefty man, tapping his foot to the tune the orchestra was playing, and a woman with a huge hoop-skirt. The seats were only wooden chairs, not like the comfortable movie-theater seats Jonathan was used to.

Craning his neck, Jonathan surveyed the audience on the main floor. They were mostly adults, with a few kids here and there, like a girl about his age in this row. No sign of Matt or Emily. Should he go check the balcony, or backstage?

"Look, Maggie." The woman beside him spoke to the girl, pointing across the theater. "That's the president's box, up there next to the stage, draped with flags."

The girl squirmed with excitement. "Oh, Mama, will we see President Lincoln?"

"Indeed, and perhaps General Grant," promised her mother. "Keep your eye fastened on the box!"

Better to stay where he was, decided Jonathan, and keep his own eye fastened on Lincoln's box. If Emily or Matt came looking for him, Jonathan, he was in plain sight. And if Lincoln did show up, he'd know right away. As for Booth, Jonathan hoped he was in a nice snug jail cell by now.

As the houselights dimmed and the curtain went up, Jonathan kept glancing up at the empty box reserved for President Lincoln. His hopes grew. Lincoln must have changed his mind, after all. Matt must have gotten Mrs. Lincoln, or maybe one of Lincoln's sons, to talk the president into staying home tonight.

The play began. It was the silliest play, Jonathan thought, that he had ever seen, about a rich Yankee who talked and acted like a cartoon hillbilly and a pushy English mother trying to marry off her daughter to him. The style of the play reminded him of one of those old sixties sitcoms that his sister, Grace, watched sometimes. A character in the play would say something that was supposed to be funny. There would be a long pause, while the actors waited and the audience laughed, as reliable as a laugh track on TV. Then another minute or so of action, and another "funny" line.

Bor-ing, thought Jonathan. He slumped down in his seat, although these straight wooden chairs weren't very good for slumping. And then, staring at the stage, he pulled himself up. There was a familiar face behind the footlights, a face framed with clusters of red corkscrew curls.

"Emily!" exclaimed Jonathan. The people on each side of him frowned and shushed him. He leaned back. At least now he knew where Emily was. She seemed to be having a great time — did that mean her mission to get Booth arrested had succeeded? Look at her mugging it up, with eyes wide and hand over her mouth. Her curls bounced like Slinkies.

There was a buzz in the audience, heads turning toward the right. The mother next to Jonathan nudged her daughter and pointed up at the president's box. At the sight of the long, kindly, bearded face, Jonathan's heart sank. So Matt's mission with the Lincoln family had failed.

The orchestra struck up "Hail to the Chief," and the audience stood and applauded. President Lincoln bowed and smiled, while Mrs. Lincoln nodded graciously. Then the Lincolns and the younger couple with them sat down.

"Is that General and Mrs. Grant, Mama?" whispered the girl. "No, no," her mother whispered back. "The Grants are much older, and that officer is only a major."

President Lincoln was out of Jonathan's line of sight now, behind one of the flags. He could see part of Mrs. Lincoln's black-and-white dress, standing out against the red sofa.

The play went on, but now Jonathan was only waiting for intermission. As soon as the house lights went up, he edged past the lady's hoopskirt and her daughter's hoopskirt. Wiggling his way down the aisle through an obstacle course of more full skirts and walking sticks, he hurried up the steps to the stage.

Fortunately, Emily was right there in the wings, chatting with a stagehand. "Jonathan!" She pulled him aside and spoke in a low voice. "Did it work? Did you get John Wilkes Booth arrested?"

Jonathan shook his head, feeling his hopes sink. "I was going to ask you the same thing. Have you seen Matt?"

"No," Emily said.

"Me neither."

A woman swept up to them, her yellow silk dress rustling. "Emily, what are you thinking of? You must change for the dairy scene." She gave Jonathan a look that said, Get lost, or I'll have you thrown out.

"I'll look for Matt," whispered Jonathan.

"I'll stay here, in case you-know-what," Emily whispered back as he ducked around the curtain.

Back in the aisle of the theater, Jonathan realized it wasn't Matt he should look for — it was John Wilkes Booth. He wove his way through the still-crowded aisle and across the lobby to the door. "Excuse me, sir," he said to the ticket taker. "Have you seen Mr. John Wilkes Booth?"

"And what if I have?" asked the man, looking Jonathan up and down. "Do you have important business with him?" He chuckled.

"Yes, as a matter of fact," said Jonathan without smiling.

The man shrugged good-naturedly. "He'll be back before long — he only went to the saloon next door."

"Thanks." Jonathan felt cold. So Booth *was* here, running around loose. Secretary of War

Stanton's man couldn't have kept a very watchful eye on the actor.

Then a new idea struck Jonathan, and he turned and headed for the stairs. He'd warned Lincoln about the assassination plot, but he hadn't warned his bodyguard, Mr. Crook. Why hadn't he thought of that when he met Crook in Lincoln's office?

Upstairs, Jonathan hurried behind the half-circle of the balcony. All the way past the rows of seats, there was a white door. That door must lead to the box on this side — the president's box! A man sat in a chair outside the door. Two other men lounged against the wall, talking.

"Excuse me," Jonathan asked them, "have you seen Mr. Crook, the president's bodyguard?

"Crook's not on duty tonight," said the man in the chair. He had a pleasant, easygoing face.

"Well, are you the bodyguard for tonight, then?" asked Jonathan.

This question got a laugh from all three men. "Pistol-packin' Forbes, they call you," teased one of them, twirling his luxuriant mustache. "Mr. Forbes is a White House footman," explained the other to Jonathan.

Trying to keep his patience, Jonathan kept asking questions. He found out that Forbes *couldn't* guard the president; he didn't have a gun. The guard for tonight, "that new fellow, Parker," had "stepped next door." Forbes put his hand, holding an imaginary glass, to his lips, as if he were tossing down a drink.

Slowly Jonathan walked back around the balcony. Things were looking worse and worse. The faithful Crook was off duty. His replacement was in the saloon next door, drinking — maybe clinking glasses with the assassin himself! — when he ought to be guarding the president with his life. There was nobody between Booth and Lincoln except an unarmed footman.

But Parker would come back soon, wouldn't he? Then Jonathan could warn him. Jonathan hung around behind the balcony, watching the audience trickle back into their seats. The houselights dimmed and the curtain rose. *Our American Cousin* began again. But no one walked past Jonathan to take up guard duty outside the president's box.

Finally, spotting in the audience the two men who'd been chatting with Forbes, Jonathan stooped down beside their row. "Psst! Sir — you with the big mustache — did you see Mr. Parker come back?"

"Shh!" said several people to Jonathan. The audience laughed at something in the play. The mustached man turned to Jonathan, looking annoyed. "That's Parker over there, at the end of that row, with the sideburns. Go make a nuisance of yourself to him!"

Walking down the aisle, Jonathan stooped beside a man with frizzy whiskers. "Shouldn't you be guarding the president?"

The man started and half-rose from his seat, then sank back down as he saw that Jonathan was only a boy. "Hang your impertinence!" His breath was heavy with hard liquor. "None of *your* affair, but Mr. Lincoln himself told me to go enjoy the play."

"There's a plot to kill the president tonight. Right here. Like, very soon," Jonathan urged. "Please, go back to the box."

The audience around Jonathan and Parker shushed and threw them angry glances. At first Parker seemed determined to ignore Jonathan. But Jonathan kept pestering him, making sure he couldn't settle down to enjoy the play. Then Parker threatened to call an usher. And then Jonathan threatened to tell Secretary of War Stanton that Parker was neglecting his duty.

That did it. Parker grumbled and stirred as if he might, after all, get up.

Out of the corner of his eye, Jonathan thought he glimpsed a dark figure gliding through the shadows above the balcony. He turned, but now there was no one up there behind the rows of seats. He yanked on Parker's arm. "Move it!"

Locked in the dusty wardrobe in the room on the third floor of the Herndon House, Matt had plenty of time to think over what he'd done wrong. He should have run to get the police the minute he heard Booth and his henchmen talking over their plans. He had no business taking chances like this — hadn't he told Emily it was too dangerous?

Matt drew back his cramped arms and legs as far as he could and then lurched forward, thumping his shoulder against the wardrobe door. No use. It was sturdy wood, and the lock wasn't any flimsy decoration, either. If only he'd brought his Swiss Army knife, he might have been able to gouge his way out of here before ten o'clock. "Help!" he yelled. "Let me out!"

Of course, maybe Jonathan had succeeded in talking the president out of going to the theater tonight. If Lincoln didn't show, Lewis and George wouldn't know about it. They'd go ahead with their assignments, trying to kill Secretary of State Seward and Vice President Johnson. Then the plot would be discovered, and Booth would be arrested, or at least would have to leave town. And Lincoln would be saved.

But somehow Matt couldn't really imagine that scenario. The image that filled his mind was John Wilkes Booth in his black villain's suit, riding toward Ford's Theater with a fancy little deadly pistol in his coat pocket. And President Lincoln — Tad's father — leaning back in his

117

carriage as he looked forward to watching the play. Somehow Matt had to stop these two men's paths from meeting.

Much later, after Matt had yelled himself hoarse and thumped his shoulder until it was sore, a maid finally heard him and unlocked the wardrobe. Matt scrambled out with thanks but no explanation, and stumbled downstairs with cramped leg muscles. In the lobby, a clock behind the desk showed almost 9:45.

If that clock was right, there was still time. Matt pelted along the streets, tripping over cobblestones and splashing through puddles. The night sky had cleared, except for a few clouds sliding across the stars.

Tenth Street in front of Ford's Theater was quiet, with only a few carriages waiting. *It hadn't happened yet.* At the door the ticket taker put out his hand, but Matt ducked under the man's arm and dashed up the stairs. He ran around the back of the balcony, gasping for breath. The audience was laughing, but Matt hadn't heard the fateful "funniest line in the play" yet.

At the door to the president's box, Matt stopped short. Jonathan and a man with sideburns and a flushed face were both pounding on the door. Another man, wearing a servant's uniform, stood by with his arms hanging. "Mr.

Booth showed me his card," he was saying. "The president *wanted* to meet him."

Jonathan turned toward Matt, staring blankly, as if he'd never seen his friend before, or as if it didn't matter who he was. He gave the white door one more thump and groaned, "Jammed from inside!"

Backstage after intermission, Emily let the costume lady button her into a pink-flowered dress with a sash and bow in back. Then she stood in the wings, waiting for her entrance and peering out at the audience. It was hard to make out any one person in the darkened house, but she thought she caught sight of Jonathan's long, skinny form moving around up in the balcony. Where was Matt? He'd failed to keep Lincoln away from the theater, but had he somehow prevented John Wilkes Booth from getting here?

There was no way for Emily to know. She'd just have to wait and watch. She'd be ready to charge onstage at the last minute and shout out her warning.

For now, Emily stepped in front of the footlights with the other actors, making the exaggerated expressions and gestures Laura Keene had coached her in. Then she followed the ladies offstage, with an extra flounce.

"Very nice, my dear," whispered Miss Keene.

She beamed at Emily through her heavy stage makeup. "We may have a place for you in the company, after tonight."

Emily made herself beam back. She stayed in the wings, watching. The funniest line was very close, now. Her chest tightened.

On stage, Augusta's pushy mother, Mrs. Mountchessington, was giving a piece of her mind to the rich Yankee who didn't want to marry her daughter. Mrs. Mountchessington bore down on the Yankee with lifted chin, making ridiculously grand gestures. Now she was sweeping off the stage. Laughter rippled across the audience.

Now Mr. Hawk, playing the Yankee, would say the funniest line in the play. There would be a big laugh, almost enough noise to cover a pistol shot.

No!

Emily ran onto the stage, deliberately bumping Mr. Hawk just as he was drawing breath for his "funniest line." He stared at her, too startled to ad-lib. Emily hardly noticed. She gazed over the footlights, up to the box where President Lincoln sat in a rocking chair. His plump wife, beside him on the sofa, was holding his hand.

"Watch out, Mr. Lincoln!" Emily shouted. She glimpsed a movement behind the rocking chair, deep in the shadow. "Look behind you!"

Mr. Hawk grabbed Emily by the arm and

started to steer her offstage. He'd finally thought of an ad-lib, something about how consarned crazy these British females were, even the little gals.

Emily kept her eyes fixed on the president's box. To her horror, he wasn't looking behind him. He was leaning forward, looking at *her*. So were Mrs. Lincoln and the young couple in the box. None of them looked alarmed — only mildly puzzled about what was happening onstage.

"Behind you!" Emily screamed.

Bang!

President Lincoln slumped forward, his face down. A cloud of smoke drifted over him. The young officer in the box jumped up from his chair and — finally — turned around. The figure in black lunged out of the smoke, and a knife flashed.

Mr. Hawk, still gripping Emily's arm, had frozen onstage. As they watched, Booth hurled himself over the railing of the box. His spur caught on one of the flags, and he landed awkwardly, with a grimace.

But John Wilkes Booth didn't drop his blood-smeared knife. He faced the audience, as if *he* were the hero of this play. *"Sic semper tyrannis!"* he yelled.

From the president's box came an answering scream, a woman's anguished voice. "Stop that man!"

10.
Hopeless

*B*ang!
   Jonathan jerked, as if he'd been shot himself. Matt groaned. Parker, the bodyguard, stopped hammering on the door of the box. His pink, side-whiskered face looked baffled. "That was a pistol," he said.

In the audience, a stunned silence was changing into murmurs, then shouts. From the balcony a couple of army officers hurried up to the box door. "Out of the way, boys. We'll break the door down."

"It's jammed from inside," Matt said grimly, but they paid no attention. They took turns ramming the door with their shoulders.

"Emily," gasped Matt suddenly. He grabbed Jonathan's arm. "We have to get out of here, find Emily, leave." Matt dashed around the back of the balcony, and Jonathan followed. But their path was blocked by a thickening crowd. In the rising babble of voices, only a few distinct words rang out: "Shot! The president is shot! Shot?" A stream of men was starting to flow up the stairs.

Peering over heads to the brightly lit stage, Jonathan said, "I don't see her." Actors and stagehands were scurrying back and forth in front of the scenery, and people from the audience were clambering up over the footlights. But there was no sign of Emily's red hair.

On the floor of the theater, words rippled across the crowd: "Booth! Stop Booth!" And then, "Hang Booth! Hang the actors! Hang them, hang them!" Here and there a chair splintered, giving way under the jostling crush of people.

Jonathan pulled on Matt's collar. "This is no use. Listen, let's go back to the box and see what happens." As Matt turned with a baffled face, Jonathan explained, "Maybe we did make just enough difference. Maybe he's only wounded a little bit, or — "

Matt shook his head. "I don't think so. But even if you're right, we still have to find Emily *now*."

"Okay, okay. But we can't get through this way. I noticed another door down there." He jerked his head in the direction of the box.

Moving with the surge of the crowd now, Jonathan and Matt pushed their way back. As they reached the door to the president's box, it opened suddenly. There stood the young officer who had come with the Lincolns, so white-faced that Jonathan hardly recognized him. His coat sleeve was ripped from shoulder to elbow, soaked with blood. "Is there a surgeon in the house?"

"Let me through!" commanded a man in the crowd behind the boys. "I am a surgeon. Let me through to the president."

The crowd squeezed aside to let the surgeon into the box. Jonathan longed to stay and hear the news. Maybe, just maybe, it would be good news. But Matt yanked him on toward the other door. "Quick!"

The door was unlocked. As Matt and Jonathan hurried into a dark corridor, there was the rustle of silk, and a woman holding a candle appeared at the top of a narrow staircase. It was the same woman Jonathan had seen backstage, telling Emily what to do.

"I must go to the president," she gasped, more to herself than the boys. As her wide skirts brushed past them, Jonathan saw that her stage makeup was smeared. Her face was strained and grim, much older than she'd looked in the play.

Clattering down the stairs, the boys found themselves in a saloon. There was a small crowd of men in here, straggling toward the front door, arguing and shouting. "Is the president alive?" "Booth? Impossible!" "Hang him!"

"This way," said Matt, nodding toward the empty back end of the bar. "There must be a door to the alley."

Sure enough, the back hall led to a door that opened onto an alley. At the theater next door, light from the stage door shone into a courtyard. A group of men were gathered around a teenage boy, lying on the ground.

"Who was it?" demanded one of the men.

"Mr. Booth. He kicked me." The boy's moan had a hurt and baffled tone. "I was just holdin' his mare for him, like he tole me. I didn't do nothin'! He come running out" — he pointed to the backstage door — "and grabbed the reins, and *kicked* me!"

"And then he rode off?" the man asked. The boy nodded in a dazed way.

Jonathan and Matt hurried around the group in the courtyard and ran up the back steps of the theater. Inside, people were rushing around every which way among the ropes and curtains and scenery. Matt grabbed a stagehand by the sleeve. "Have you seen Emily, a girl with red hair?"

The man pulled away. "The president is shot!" He hurried on, like an ant from a dug-up nest.

Jonathan and Matt pushed on through the wings to the stage. Someone with heavy boots stepped on Jonathan's foot, and someone else bumped his nose with an elbow. The crowd was up on the stage, too, but mostly on one side. People shoved each other to get a better view of the president's box, yelled up at the box, even tried to climb up to its railing.

On the other side of the stage, Jonathan and Matt shaded their eyes to peer over the footlights. "I hope she's not down there," Matt said grimly.

The crowd on the floor of the theater was moving like a monster amoeba, struggling toward the door. At the same time, people caught in the crowd were trying to shove their way to one side of the theater or the other, or back toward the stage. They groaned and screamed. "Kill the actors! Burn the theater!" Beneath the uproar there was the shuffling of hundreds and hundreds of feet. And above the din a child's voice piped: "Papa — Papa — *Papa!*"

"This is my fault," said Matt in a choked voice. "If she's down there, she could get trampled." He started toward the steps that led from the stage to the floor.

"No!" Jonathan grabbed his friend's arm. An idea came to him. "Listen, Emily's not stupid. She wouldn't try to get out that way. She'd go out the back and around."

"Maybe you're right." Matt paused, looking relieved. "She'd try to meet us out in the street, because that's where we have to leave from, anyway."

The boys retraced their way through the backstage and out the stage door, then ran down the alley and around to Tenth Street.

As they struggled through the crowded street, soldiers appeared at the top of the theater steps, pushing aside the throng. Yellow light from a lamppost fell on a double line of men inching out of one of the archways, carrying something long.

"Does the president live?" called out a strained voice from the crowd. Jonathan's mind picked up the last word. *Live, live, let him live.*

One of the soldiers called back, "Yes, but not for long. It is hopeless."

Hopeless. The answer bored through Jonathan, more final than the pistol shot.

"Hopeless. Hopeless!" echoed through the crowd, and the screams and moans grew louder. Jonathan thought he was going to smother. He felt desperate to get away.

"Man, I want to get out of here," said Matt in Jonathan's ear. "Emily, show up!"

"Yeah, but we're stuck." Jonathan groaned. "These people aren't going to go away. And isn't that about the spot for our picture, where that wagon is?"

Even as Jonathan pointed to a flatbed wagon loaded with barrels, a girl with red curls climbed onto the wagon from the opposite side. She stood up, steadying herself with one hand on a barrel, and gazed around at the crowd. "Emily!" exclaimed Jonathan and Matt together.

It took them a few minutes to work their way through the crush, past the stamping, nervous horses, to the wagon. The driver, talking soothingly to his horses, looked over his shoulder as Matt and Jonathan clambered onto the flatbed. "Hey, there! Get down. Stay out of them barrels."

Emily stepped up to the driver's seat, whispered something to him, and dropped something into his hand. Then she hurried back to the boys and gave Matt a fierce hug. "I was afraid — I thought you might have tried something — "

"I did," admitted Matt. "I'll tell you about it later."

"What did you say to the driver?" Jonathan asked Emily.

"I gave him the money Miss Keene owed me for being in the play tonight," said Emily. "I told him we just wanted a place to stand for a minute. Because isn't this where we're supposed to stand, for the TASC to bring us back?"

Matt glanced from one side of the street to the other. "You're exactly right. We were in front of the middle archway."

"Not *exactly* right," Jonathan said drily. It was unbelievable, how Emily and Matt had no idea of scientific precision. "We're about four feet off the ground."

Emily wasn't listening to him. She gasped and pointed across the crowd, at the cluster of men

128

carrying President Lincoln down the theater steps.

"Where can we take him?" the man supporting Lincoln's head called over his shoulder.

"Bring him in here!" A man beckoned from across the street, standing on the high front steps of a brick house.

"That's the house where Lincoln is going to die," said Matt softly. "It's time for us to leave."

"No!" Jonathan burst out. "You don't *know* he's — Maybe — " Realizing he wasn't making sense, he tried to pull himself together. "We can't go until the street clears," he went on in his most matter-of-fact, scientific voice. "See, at this height, eighty percent of us would be out of the picture."

Grabbing Jonathan by both arms, Matt looked into his eyes. "Listen, Schultz. We have to go. It's not like we can stay at a motel for a few days until the street clears."

"Hurry," urged Emily. "Before the wagon moves. We can crawl *under* it." As Jonathan gave her a surprised glance, she added, "Couldn't the TASC pick us up, even with all the people around?"

Squeezing his eyes shut, Jonathan let out a deep sigh. Of course Matt and Emily were right about leaving now. Their mission was over; it was dangerous to stay, especially in the middle of this frantic crowd. The only question was whether the TASC would work right with all these extra people, to say nothing of the wagon, on the edges of the "picture." "Probably," he answered Emily.

Emily leaned over to the driver. "Please don't move the wagon for about five minutes, all right?"

"Five minutes!" said the driver gruffly. He pushed up the brim of his hat and glared at the crush of people all around the wagon. "You might as well say five hours."

"Thanks," breathed Emily.

Matt shrugged off his jacket and dropped it onto the driver's seat. "Give this to some boy who needs it, okay?"

One after the other, the three kids climbed down from the wagon and squeezed in between the wheels. "I hope we're really in the right place," Jonathan muttered. Now that they were crouching under the wagon, it seemed to be moving more, with a lot of creaking.

"Just do it," urged Matt.

Jonathan tugged the TASC remote control out of his pants pocket. In the dark under the wagon, he couldn't see the buttons, but he knew them by feel. "Get together. Hold still! Ready for TRANSPORT."

The three kids crouched in a line under the length of the wagon, their shoulders touching. Jonathan couldn't see anything beyond the wagon except boots and skirt hems. The noise of the crowd had shifted from screaming and cursing to sobbing and moaning. A child's thin voice — Jonathan hoped it wasn't the same little kid as before — wailed, "Papa? Papa? *Papa!*"

11.
Glory, Hallelujah!

The next morning, Monday, Jonathan woke up thinking that something terrible had happened.

He was right: President Lincoln had been shot. How could he get out of bed and go to school, just as if nothing was wrong?

Somehow, Jonathan did get up and drag himself through the school day. A couple of times he caught sight of Matt in the halls. They didn't get a chance to talk, but Jonathan thought his friend looked dazed, too.

Back home that afternoon, Jonathan lay on his bed, staring across the room at his iguana. The iguana stared back. Neither of them moved. This was normal for the iguana, but not for Jonathan. His room was full of things he'd ordinarily be doing something with: his stereo, his books, his computer. And of course the TASC, sitting in a corner with a sheet thrown over it, like a ghost.

The phone rang in the kitchen. Nobody else was home. Rolling off his bed, Jonathan plodded out to the phone.

It was Matt. "Hey. We've got the money — Emily's and my share of the remote."

"Oh, that," said Jonathan. He'd forgotten that his sister, Grace, had made him go to Radio Shack yesterday afternoon and buy a new remote control for the TV. "Never mind."

"No — we owe you. Meet you in the park in fifteen minutes, okay?"

A short while later, Jonathan paused at the top of the park, a hill overlooking the river. Out in the sunshine, he felt a little better. The breeze, blowing uphill across the park, smelled like grass and some kind of heavy-scented flowers — lilacs.

Jonathan caught sight of Matt and Emily in shorts and T-shirts, appearing through a row of pine trees at the bottom of the park. He hurried down the path toward them — and then stopped short as he came upon a park bench. It was the same bench where he and Matt and Emily had rested the cartons full of TASC parts, three days ago. "Hi, Mr. Kenny," he said to the man sitting on the bench.

Emily and Matt came up to the bench, too. "Oh — hi, Grandpa," said Emily. She sat down beside the old man, and he put his arm around her. "Did your neighbors give you a ride up here?" she asked.

Mr. Kenny nodded, gazing out over the river from under the bill of his baseball cap. "They know I like to sit up here in good weather. Yep, I like to sit here and think about the things that've happened on the Hudson River. In the Revolution, we had a big chain stretched across the river at West Point. That kept the British warships from sailing up." Pausing, the old man looked over at Emily, then up at Matt and Jonathan. " 'Course, President Lincoln's funeral train came up along this river, too."

"Oh, really?" asked Matt. He put his hands in his pockets, took them out, and put them in again, as if he were wondering whether his great-grandfather suspected anything. Jonathan wondered, too.

"That's right," said Mr. Kenny. "The funeral train went north from Washington to New York City, then up the Hudson to Albany. Then west all the way to Springfield, Illinois. That's where they buried him."

Down at the railroad station by the river, a train paused, then slid upriver along the tracks. In Jonathan's mind, the sleek Amtrak train below became a steam locomotive, trailing smoke from its top-heavy funnel. Music seemed to start up inside his head. It was "The Battle Hymn of the Republic," the victory song that Jonathan

134

and a bunch of men had sung in Harvey's Oyster Saloon. Now the same tune sounded slow and solemn — a funeral march.

"Grandpa." Emily was giving her great-grandfather a cautious sideways glance. "Speaking of Lincoln, one thing I don't get about John Wilkes Booth — "

"What's to get?" snorted the old man. "He had bats in his belfry, that character."

"I mean I didn't get something he said." Noticing Jonathan and Matt glaring at her in horror, Emily turned pink. "Of course I didn't *hear* him say it."

Jonathan groaned inwardly.

"I must have read it somewhere," Emily went on, glaring back at the boys. "But wasn't it in another language — what Booth shouted, when he jumped down from Lincoln's box?"

"*Sic semper tyrannis,*" growled the old man.

"I know what that means," Matt said. "Like, 'This is what's always going to happen — should happen — to tyrants.' As if Lincoln was a tyrant!"

"Touched in the head." Mr. Kenny tapped the side of his own blue-veined forehead. "Booth thought killing President Lincoln would help the South. But the South would have been much better off if Lincoln had lived."

Jonathan exchanged glances with Matt and Emily, then squinted down at the old man. He couldn't tell anything from the expression on the deeply creased face. Was Mr. Kenny playing games with the three kids, chatting about Lincoln like this? Did he suspect they'd stolen the TASC cartons and traveled to 1865?

"When you think about it," Mr. Kenny went on in his gravelly voice, "Abraham Lincoln was lucky, luckier than most. He accomplished his mission in life — he held the Union together."

"And he freed the slaves," put in Emily.

Remembering President Lincoln's worn, patient face, Jonathan thought, Mr. Kenny's right. Lincoln was pretty sure someone was going to kill him, sooner or later. He just wanted to live long enough to pull the country through the war.

Jonathan's chest ached; his throat ached; his eyes stung. At the same time, the details of the scene around him became very sharp. The blades of grass in the lawn, the pattern of the bark on the trees, the white flecks of sailboats on the river below, all seemed to stand out.

Jonathan opened his mouth to say what he was thinking about Lincoln, but Matt spoke first. "*So,* I guess we'd better be going." He nudged his sister's sneaker with his foot. "Where's the money we owe Jonathan for — uh — breaking the remote?"

"Oh, right." Jumping to her feet, Emily pulled a wad of dollar bills from her shorts pocket and held it out to Jonathan. "Well, see you later, Grandpa."

Changing his mind about speaking, Jonathan followed Matt and Emily down the path. When the three kids were far enough from the old man, Matt hissed, "What's the matter with you guys? I thought you'd never stop going on about Lincoln. Couldn't you see he suspected? Couldn't you tell he was trying to trip us up?"

Emily lifted her chin defiantly. "You and Jonathan didn't have to *stare* at me when I said that about Booth. That gave it away more than what I said, you know."

"And you, Cowen." Jonathan pointed a finger at Matt. "Why'd *you* have to even mention the remote? That was a giant clue that we'd taken the cartons, because Mr. Kenny knew the TASC remote wasn't in them. He knew if we were going to use the TASC again, I'd have to construct another remote."

The three kids exchanged scowls. Then Jonathan grinned and shrugged. "Okay, he suspects. But he doesn't know. And besides, he wasn't that mad."

Halfway to the row of pine trees at the bottom of the park, the kids turned and looked up the hill toward the bench. Mr. Kenny was still sitting there, a little smile on his face. He raised one hand in a gesture that might mean, See you later. Or, it might mean, You couldn't save Lincoln, but I know you gave it a good try.

"I guess he *isn't* mad," Matt admitted. "So, where are we going now?"

Jonathan and Emily gave him startled looks. Emily burst out, "Isn't it a little soon to plan our next trip?"

Exactly what Jonathan had thought. But Matt started to laugh. "I didn't mean, Where to in the past!"

Jonathan laughed, too, and patted the bunch of dollar bills in his pocket. "We're going to the diner, that's where. I'm rich!" He took a flying leap down the hill.

"To the diner!" echoed Matt behind him. "Glory, hallelujah!"

"Glory, glory, hallelujah!" Emily sang breathlessly.

Glancing over his shoulder, Jonathan saw them leaping after him, flapping their arms as they bounded downhill. "Glory, glory, hallelujah!" he continued the song. "Those fries are mighty good!"

Floating in long-legged strides ahead of his friends, Jonathan felt as if he were going to take off.